LIBRARY
TELLURIDE M/
725 W COL
TELLURIDE, C

D0056818

DATE DUE

The Library Store #47-0152

Match Wits with Super Sleuth Nancy Drew!

Collect the Original
Nancy Drew Mystery Stories®
by Carolyn Keene

Available in Hardcover!

The Secret of the Old Clock
The Hidden Staircase
The Bungalow Mystery
The Mystery at Lilac Inn
The Secret of Shadow Ranch
The Secret of Red Gate Farm
The Clue in the Diary
Nancy's Mysterious Letter
The Sign of the Twisted Candles
Password to Larkspur Lane
The Clue of the Broken Locket
The Message in the Hollow Oak
The Mystery of the Ivory Charm
The Whispering Statue
The Haunted Bridge
The Clue of the Tapping Heels
The Mystery of the Brass-Bound
  Trunk
The Mystery of the Moss-Covered
  Mansion
The Quest of the Missing Map
The Clue in the Jewel Box
The Secret in the Old Attic
The Clue in the Crumbling Wall
The Mystery of the Tolling Bell
The Clue in the Old Album
The Ghost of Blackwood Hall
The Clue of the Leaning Chimney
The Secret of the Wooden Lady

The Clue of the Black Keys
Mystery at the Ski Jump
The Clue of the Velvet Mask
The Ringmaster's Secret
The Scarlet Slipper Mystery
The Witch Tree Symbol
The Hidden Window Mystery
The Haunted Showboat
The Secret of the Golden Pavilion
The Clue in the Old Stagecoach
The Mystery of the Fire Dragon
The Clue of the Dancing Puppet
The Moonstone Castle Mystery
The Clue of the Whistling Bagpipes
The Phantom of Pine Hill
The Mystery of the 99 Steps
The Clue in the Crossword Cipher
The Spider Sapphire Mystery
The Invisible Intruder
The Mysterious Mannequin
The Crooked Banister
The Secret of Mirror Bay
The Double Jinx Mystery
Mystery of the Glowing Eye
The Secret of the Forgotten City
The Sky Phantom
Strange Message in the Parchment
Mystery of Crocodile Island
The Thirteenth Pearl

Nancy Drew Back-to-Back
The Secret of the Old Clock/ The Hidden Staircase

Celebrate 60 Years with the World's Best Detective!

The Secret of Red Gate Farm

If only there was enough time to copy the code!

The Secret of Red Gate Farm

BY CAROLYN KEENE

GROSSET & DUNLAP
Publishers • New York
A member of The Putnam & Grosset Group

PRINTED ON RECYCLED PAPER

Copyright © 1989, 1961, 1931 by Simon & Schuster, Inc. All rights reserved.
Published by Grosset & Dunlap, Inc., a member of The Putnam &
Grosset Group, New York. Published simultaneously in Canada. Printed in the U.S.A.
NANCY DREW MYSTERY STORIES® is a registered trademark of Simon & Schuster, Inc
GROSSET & DUNLAP is a trademark of Grosset & Dunlap, Inc.
ISBN 0-448-09506-8
2000 Printing

Contents

The Secret of Red Gate Farm

CHAPTER I

A Strange Fragrance

"THAT Oriental-looking clerk in the perfume shop certainly acted mysterious," Bess Marvin declared, as she and her two friends ended their shopping trip and hurried down the street to the railroad station.

"Yes," Nancy Drew answered thoughtfully. "I wonder why she didn't want you to buy that bottle of Blue Jade?"

"The price would have discouraged me," spoke up Bess's cousin, dark-haired George Fayne. Her boyish name fitted her slim build and straightforward, breezy manner. "Twenty dollars an ounce!"

Blond, pretty Bess, who had a love for feminine luxuries, laughed. "I *was* extravagant, but I just couldn't resist such yummy perfume. After all, Dad gave me money to buy something frivolous, so I did!"

1

Nancy by this time was some distance ahead. "Hurry, girls, or we'll miss the next train to River Heights!" In her active life the attractive, titian-haired young sleuth had learned that being on time was important.

The three eighteen-year-old girls continued their frantic pace until the railroad station finally came into view.

Once at the station, they set down their packages to rest their arms. "Whew!" Bess sighed, looking at her watch. "I didn't think we'd make it, but we have two minutes to spare. And this would be one of July's hottest days!"

Nancy was pensive, still contemplating their encounter with the mysterious woman in the Oriental perfume shop. She had realized the Blue Jade was much too expensive, and the unwillingness of the young woman to part with it had stimulated her interest. Instinct had told Nancy that there must be some special reason why the saleswoman had been so reluctant to sell the Blue Jade.

Then another idea struck her. "You know," she said aloud, "it's possible that saleswoman deliberately raised the price of the perfume."

George frowned. "But why? You'd think she'd be thrilled to make such a good sale."

"Yes," Nancy agreed. "That's what perplexes me. There's something very strange about it and I'd certainly like to know what it is!"

"Oh, Nancy," teased George, "there you go again, dreaming up another mystery!"

Nancy's blue eyes sparkled as she thought of the prospect. The young sleuth had already solved several mysteries, some of them for her father, Carson Drew, a famous criminal lawyer. Among the cases on which Nancy had worked were *The Secret in the Old Clock* and *The Secret of Shadow Ranch*.

The girls heard the train approaching the station. As it came to a halt they quickly gathered up their packages and hurried aboard.

"What a day!" Bess exclaimed as she pushed on through the cars. The train was crowded, and the girls walked through several cars before they found any vacant seats.

George and Bess began discussing their many purchases. Bess gloated in particular over the bottle of exotic perfume. Even though the package was wrapped, it gave off a slight fragrance which was very pleasant.

George took a quick inventory of their purchases, then laughed. "Bess, it's a good thing we got you to leave that last department store or you wouldn't have had enough money left to buy your ticket home," she stated bluntly. "You should practice self-control, the way I do."

"Self-control!" Bess retorted. "I suppose you call a new hat, two dresses, three pairs of stockings, and a handbag self-control!"

George mustered a smile and decided to drop the subject.

Nancy leaned her head back against the cushion, and as she relaxed, studied the faces of the nearby passengers. She thought that the thin, sweet-looking girl who occupied the seat just opposite looked very tired, worried, and even ill. Nancy judged the girl to be her own age.

"Why are you so quiet, Nancy?" Bess demanded suddenly.

"Just resting," Nancy returned.

She did not tell her friends that she had become interested in the nearby passenger, for George and Bess often teased her about her habit of scrutinizing strange faces. However, it was Nancy's lively interest in people that was largely responsible for involving her in unusual adventures, and she was always on the alert for a new mystery.

Bess eyed her perfume package longingly and finally ripped off the paper. "I can't stand it any longer." She sighed. "I must try some of this delicious-smelling stuff!" She opened the bottle and dabbed a couple of drops behind each ear. Then she offered it to George. "Try some. It's really lovely—makes me think I'm in the mystic Orient."

George could not keep from making a face. "No *thank* you!" she replied firmly. "It's not my type!"

Nancy and Bess laughed. Then Bess offered some to Nancy, who accepted willingly. Bess again took out the stopper and was leaning over to put some perfume on Nancy when the train lurched and jogged her arm.

"Oh!" Bess cried in horror. The perfume sprayed over Nancy, as the bottle fell to the floor.

"Such a waste of money!" George muttered as she picked up the half-empty container.

"What a shame!" Nancy exclaimed. "It's your perfume, Bess, and now I have a lot of it on me."

Bess groaned. "I should've waited till I was home to open the bottle. I'm lucky there's some left!" Carefully she placed the small vial in her handbag.

By now the concentrated odor of Blue Jade had permeated the car, and passengers in nearby seats flung open the windows.

"I'm glad we're getting off at the next stop." Nancy giggled. "Everyone is laughing at us."

Nancy had become so engrossed with the spilled perfume that she had forgotten about the pale young woman who occupied the opposite seat. Now, as Nancy turned her head, she was startled to see that the girl had slumped down in a dejected heap.

"She's fainted!" Nancy exclaimed, moving quickly across the aisle.

She shook the girl gently, but there was no response from the frail figure.

"Bess! Ask if there is a doctor in the car!" Nancy cried urgently.

By this time other passengers in the car were aware that something had happened, and were crowding about, asking unnecessary questions and getting in the way. Nancy politely asked them to move back.

There did not appear to be a doctor in the coach, but as Nancy rubbed the girl's wrists, she was relieved to see that she was showing signs of recovering consciousness.

George quickly raised the window so that the fresh air fanned the girl's face. Leaning against the seat, she looked deathly pale.

"What can I do?" George asked.

"Stay here while I get some water," Nancy answered. "She's coming around now. I think she'll be all right in a few minutes."

Nancy hurried to the water cooler at the far end of the car. As she was trying to fill the paper cup, a man who had been standing near the doorway came toward her. He made a pretense of waiting his turn to get a drink, yet she realized by the intent look on his face that something had startled him. He was deliberately studying her! Was it because of the perfume? She fairly reeked with it!

Nancy was not prepared, however, for what came next. The man edged closer to her, glanced

"She's fainted!" Nancy exclaimed

quickly about to see that no one was close by, and muttered in a guttural tone:

"Any word from the Chief?"

Nancy was taken completely by surprise. She knew she had never seen the man before, for she would not have forgotten such a cruel face. His steel-gray eyes bored straight into her. Nancy was so bewildered she could think of nothing to say.

The stranger realized at once that he had made a mistake. "Excuse me, miss. My error," he murmured, starting for the car ahead. "But that perfume— Well, never mind!"

CHAPTER II

Mysterious Numbers

NANCY stared after the stranger and wondered what he could have meant.

"Evidently he mistook me for somebody else," she thought. "But even so, his actions certainly were peculiar."

What message had he expected to receive from her? Who was the Chief? How strange that the man should speak of the perfume as though it had been the cause of his mistake!

If Nancy's mind had not been occupied with the frail girl's condition, she might have wondered more over the strange encounter. She dismissed it for the moment. Quickly filling a cup with ice water, she rushed back to George and Bess, who were giving first aid to the girl.

"Do you feel better now?" Nancy asked. "Here, drink this."

"Thank you," the girl murmured, gratefully

taking the cup. "I feel much better now," she added quietly. "It was very kind of you to help me."

"It must have been the perfume that made you faint," George declared. "A little is all right, but half a bottle is overpowering."

"I'm sure it wasn't the perfume," the girl returned quickly. "I haven't felt well since I first boarded the train early this morning."

"What a shame," Bess said. "I'll get you some more water." She soon returned with a second cup.

"By the way, Nancy"—Bess turned to her friend—"who was that man who spoke to you at the water cooler?"

"You noticed him?" Nancy asked, surprised.

"Yes," Bess said, "but I didn't recognize him."

"Nor did I," Nancy remarked. "The whole thing was quite mysterious. He simply approached me and said: 'Any word from the Chief?'"

"The Chief!" Bess and George chorused. "What Chief?"

"I have no idea," the young sleuth admitted. "But evidently it was this strange perfume that attracted his attention, or so he said."

"I wonder what the perfume could have to do with it?" Bess looked perplexed.

By this time the train was slowing down as it approached the River Heights station, and Nancy and her friends realized they must hurry or they would miss their stop.

"I'm afraid that we must interrupt this conversation and say good-by," Nancy told the girl reluctantly. "We get off at River Heights."

"River Heights!" The girl glanced anxiously out the window. "I get off here too! I had no idea we were so close."

"We'll help you," Nancy offered. "Do you really feel well enough to walk?"

"Yes, I'm all right now."

George and Bess collected the miscellaneous packages, while Nancy helped the stranger along the aisle. The girl hesitated uncertainly as she stepped from the train.

"I'm not very familiar with River Heights," she said to Nancy. "Which direction should I take to go to the center of town?"

"You're still too shaky to walk any distance," George spoke up. "Have you no friend here to meet you?"

The girl shook her head.

"Then why don't you come home for a snack with us?" Nancy suggested. "I left my car parked here by the station, and I can drive you back."

The girl started to protest, but Nancy and the others urged her on, and soon they were all settled in Nancy's blue convertible.

"I haven't even told you my name," the strange girl said, leaning back wearily. "I'm Jo-

anne Byrd. I live with my grandmother at Red
Gate Farm about ten miles from Round Valley. That's where I took the train."

Nancy introduced herself and her friends as she
started the car and headed it toward the Drew
residence in another section of the city.

"How nice it must be to live on a farm!" Bess
remarked. "And Red Gate is such a pleasant-
sounding name."

"Red Gate *is* a lovely place," Joanne said feel-
ingly. "I've lived there with my grandmother
ever since I can remember. We don't have the
money, though, to keep up the farm. That's why
I left home today—to find work here."

"Do you have something in mind?" Bess questioned.

"I came in response to a particular advertisement," Joanne replied, but did not say what it
was. A faraway look came into her eyes. "We simply must raise enough money to pay the long-
standing interest due on the mortgage of our
farm or Gram will lose it."

"Surely no one would be mean enough to take
over your farm," Bess murmured sympatheti-
cally.

"A bank holds the mortgage. It has no choice.
Gram knows very little about money matters, so
she takes anyone's advice. Years ago she was advised to buy another farm and sell it at a high
price. All at once values crashed and she couldn't

meet the payments on her extra farm, so it went back to the original owners. Then she had to put a heavy mortgage on Red Gate, too, and if she loses that, she'll be penniless."

As Joanne finished her story, Nancy turned the car into the Drews' driveway.

"Come in, everybody," she invited. "Perhaps we can think of a way to help Joanne."

The three girls followed Nancy into the house, where they were greeted by the Drews' pleasant housekeeper. Hannah Gruen had been like a mother to Nancy ever since the death of Mrs. Drew when Nancy was a child. Nancy asked Hannah to make some sandwiches for them all, then led the girls to the living room.

"You must be nearly starved," Nancy said to Joanne a moment later. "I know I am."

"I am rather hungry," Joanne confessed. "I haven't had anything to eat since last night."

"What!" the other girls chorused.

"It was my own fault," Joanne said hastily. "I was too excited this morning to think about food."

"It's no wonder you fainted," Nancy said. "I'll ask Hannah to fix you something hot."

Nancy returned from the kitchen with a tray of appetizing sandwiches and a bowl of soup. Joanne ate heartily. Nancy and her friends joined in, for they had had only a light snack while on their shopping expedition.

"I do feel better," Joanne announced when she had finished. "It was so good of you to bring me here."

"Not at all," Nancy said softly. "We'd like to help you all we can."

"Thank you, but I believe everything will work out all right if only I get this position." Joanne glanced anxiously at the clock. "I'll really have to go now or I'll be too late to make the call this afternoon. Could you tell me how to get to this address?"

She handed a folded scrap of newspaper to Nancy. "This particular ad for an office girl caught my eye since it asks for someone who has had experience on a farm."

Nancy found the advertisement to be rather conventional, but it was the name at the bottom of the paragraph that held her attention.

"Why, this ad says Riverside Heights!" she exclaimed. "You should have stayed on the train until the next stop!"

"I thought Riverside Heights and River Heights were the same place!" Joanne Byrd cried in distressed surprise.

"Riverside Heights is only a few miles away," Nancy explained, "and the names are confusing even to people who live near here, so it's a natural mistake."

"Oh, dear, I don't know what to do now," Joanne said anxiously. "If I don't apply for that position this afternoon, I'll probably lose my chance of getting it."

Nancy had taken a liking to the girl and wanted to help her. Not only was Joanne half sick from lack of food, but she had worked herself into a nervous state.

"You must let me drive you to Riverside Heights," Nancy insisted. "It'll only take fifteen minutes and you'll have plenty of time to apply for the position."

Joanne's face brightened instantly, but she was reluctant to accept the favor. "I've really troubled you enough."

"Nonsense! We'll start right away!" Nancy turned to Bess and George. "Want to come along?"

Bess and George both declined, since they were expected home. The cousins gathered up their packages and all the girls went to the car. Nancy dropped Bess and George at their own homes, then took the highway leading to the next city.

"I do hope I get there in time," Joanne said worriedly. "The job will mean so much to Gram and me!"

"You'll get there," Nancy assured her. "Have you ever applied for a job before?"

"No. I've always helped Gram run the farm until now," Joanne explained. "I felt I was more needed there than anywhere else. We keep a farm hand, but a great deal of the work still falls upon me."

The girls soon reached Riverside Heights, and Nancy had no trouble finding the address mentioned in the advertisement. It was in a run-down section of the city, but Nancy did not mention this to her companion.

"Here we are," Nancy said cheerfully, stopping the car in front of a dingy-looking office building.

Joanne made no move to get out of the car, but sat nervously pressing her hands together.

"I'm a terrible coward," she confessed. "I don't know what in the world to say when I go in. I wish you'd come with me."

"I'll be glad to," said Nancy, as she turned off the ignition and locked the car. They entered the building. There was no elevator, so the girls climbed the dimly lighted stairway to the third floor. Soon they came to Room 305, which had been mentioned in the advertisement.

"There's no name on the door," Nancy observed, "but this must be the right place."

As they stepped into the reception room, Nancy noted that it was dirty and drab. The two girls glanced at each other, exchanging expressions of disappointment.

At that moment a man came from the inner office and surveyed the girls sharply. He was tall and wiry, with hostile, penetrating eyes and harsh features. His suit was bold in pattern and color, and his necktie was gaudy.

"Well?" he demanded coldly.

Joanne found sufficient courage to take the advertisement from her pocket.

"I—I saw this in the paper," she stammered. "I came to apply for the position."

The man stared at Joanne critically, then at Nancy.

"You lookin' for the job too?" he asked.

Nancy shook her head. "No. I'm here with my friend."

The man looked at Joanne again and said with a shrug of his shoulders, "Go on in the other room. I'll talk to you in a minute."

Joanne cast Nancy a doubtful glance and obediently stepped into the inner office.

"Look here," the man addressed Nancy, "wouldn't you like that job? I could use a good-lookin' girl like you."

"I'm not looking for work, thank you," Nancy returned aloofly.

The man was about to make a retort when the telephone rang. He scowled and went over to the table to answer it. As he lifted the receiver he looked nervously back toward Nancy.

"Hello," he growled into the phone. "This is Al. Shoot!"

Nancy listened to his end of the unbusinesslike conversation and watched him reach for paper and pencil and begin to scribble down a line of figures. This in itself would not have seemed so peculiar, except that he continued to eye Nancy suspiciously.

He kept on copying figures. All the while Nancy watched him curiously.

"O.K., Hank," he muttered just before he hung up. "You say you've found a girl? . . . Fine! We can't be too careful in this business!"

All this time Nancy was wondering what kind of transactions went on in this office. There had been no indication on the door of what business the man was engaged in and nothing in the room gave her any clue. She realized now that Joanne's chances of getting the position were slim, and Nancy was actually relieved. She was very suspicious of the whole setup.

"I was just taking down some stock-market quotations," the man remarked lightly as he crossed the room toward Nancy.

"This isn't an investment house, is it?" she asked.

"No, you wouldn't call it that exactly," he answered with a smirk. "We run a manufacturing business."

"I see," Nancy murmured, though she really did not understand at all. "What do you manufacture?"

The man pretended not to hear and moved on to the inner office where Joanne was waiting. In haste to escape further questions, he forgot to pick up the sheet of paper with the numbers on it.

Nancy was curious about the telephone conversation and could not resist the temptation to take a peek at the notation. She stepped silently over to the telephone table and glanced at the sheet. Strung out across the top and bottom of the page were numbers. The top row read:

$$16\bar{5}3 \quad 112 \quad 129 \quad 156\tilde{2} \quad 16 \quad 882 \quad 091 \quad 56\underline{18}$$

"Stock quotations, like fun!" Nancy told herself. "Why did he lie about it? He must have been afraid I'd discover something!" As usual, Nancy was intrigued at any hint of a mystery. She studied the row of odd figures. Suddenly it dawned on her that they might be a message in code!

Nancy looked quickly toward the inner office. The door was open, but the man sat with his back toward her. She did not dare pick up the paper. If only there was enough time to copy the code!

With one eye on the office, Nancy took a sheet of paper and frantically scribbled the numbers, carefully keeping them in their right order. She could hear Joanne's soft voice, then her prospective employer talking loudly, and realized the interview was coming to an end.

She had copied only the top row of numbers, but dared not spend any more time at it. She put the copy into her bag and slipped back into her chair just a moment before Joanne and the man emerged from the inner room. He glanced toward the telephone, gave a start, and rushed across the room. With a muttered exclamation he grabbed the paper and thrust it into his pocket.

Nancy's heart was beating madly as she forced herself to remain outwardly calm. He stood with a cold look on his face, his eyes fixed on Nancy.

CHAPTER III

Work on a Code

HAD the man heard her rush from the telephone table? Nancy wondered. Was he suspicious of her actions during his absence? If so, what reason did he have and what business deal was he hiding in this dingy excuse for an office? Nancy pretended not to notice his penetrating, questioning eyes, but she was ill at ease.

The hostile man spoke up. "You girls better get out of here!" he blurted. "I got no more time to waste. And don't bother to come back!"

Nancy and Joanne looked hastily at each other and moved toward the door. Once outside the building, Nancy breathed a sigh of relief and turned toward Joanne, who was close to tears.

"Don't feel bad because you didn't get the job," Nancy said gently as they walked to the car. "You wouldn't have wanted it, I'm sure."

"That man was detestable!" Joanne shuddered. "I had just given my name and address when he started to shout. You must have heard him."

Nancy nodded. "I think he had already found another girl to work for him," she said. "At least I heard him say something like that over the phone."

"I knew I wouldn't get the job." Joanne sighed dejectedly. "He told me I wasn't the type!"

"I'd count my blessings if I were you," said Nancy soberly. "There's something strange going on in that office and I'd like to know what it is."

"Why, what do you mean?" Joanne asked quizzically.

"Well," Nancy began carefully, "I'm not sure my suspicions are just, but I have a hunch there's something shady about the telephone message he got when you were in the inner office." Nancy explained about the series of numbers on the sheet of paper and how she suspected they might form some sort of code.

"At any rate," Nancy went on, "we can't be sure of anything, so this must remain confidential."

Joanne nodded and fell silent.

Many thoughts raced through Nancy's mind as she remembered the day's encounters. First there had been the perfume shop and its mysterious saleswoman, then the curious man on the train who had been attracted by the strange fragrance. And now, this crude, gruff man in Room 305!

"What should I do now?" Joanne asked forlornly. "I can't go back to Red Gate Farm and let Gram down. I simply must find work!"

"Why not come home with me?" Nancy suggested as they paused beside her car. "I'll be glad to have you as my guest for the night, and in the morning you'll feel better and can decide what to do then."

Joanne shook her head proudly. "Thank you, but I wouldn't think of letting you go to any more trouble. I have a little money. I can find a boardinghouse and I'll keep on looking for work here."

Nancy saw that Joanne was disappointed and discouraged and hated to leave her on her own, but finally conceded. "I guess you're right," she admitted. "But at least let me help you hunt for a place to stay." Joanne accepted the offer gratefully.

Even with the car, it was difficult to locate a pleasant room. Joanne could not afford a high-priced place, and the cheaper ones were unsatisfactory. Finally, however, they found a suitable room on a quiet street and Nancy helped Joanne get settled.

"I may be driving over this way tomorrow," she said. "If I do, I'll stop in to see what luck you've had."

"I wish you would," Joanne invited shyly. "I'll need someone to bolster my morale."

"All right, I will," Nancy promised.

After a few words of encouragement she said good-by, then drove slowly toward River Heights, her mind again focused on the various events of the day.

"I don't know what will happen to Joanne if she doesn't find work," Nancy told herself. "It would be a shame if her grandmother loses Red Gate Farm. I wish I could do something, but I don't know of any available jobs."

It was nearly dinnertime when Nancy reached River Heights. As she passed the Fayne home, she saw George and her cousin Bess on the front lawn and stopped to tell them about Joanne's unsuccessful interview.

"Isn't that too bad?" Bess murmured in disappointment. "She seems such a sweet girl. I'd like to know her better."

"I promised I'd drive over to see her tomorrow," Nancy told the girls. "Why don't you come along?"

"Let's!" George cried enthusiastically. "I love going places with you. We always seem to find some sort of adventure!"

Nancy's blue eyes became serious. "I'd say this has been a pretty full day! I can't seem to forget that mysterious saleswoman in the Oriental perfume shop or the strange man on the train. I wasn't going to say anything to you about this, but something odd happened this afternoon in that office."

Nancy then related the mysterious actions and behavior of the man named "Al."

"You mean you think his telephone conversation was a little on the shady side?" Bess asked, wide-eyed.

"It seemed that way to me," Nancy answered. "I doubt very much that it's a manufacturing business and those numbers I copied from his pad were anything but stock-market quotations!"

"Well, here we go again! Never a dull moment with Nancy around!" George laughed gaily.

"Don't be too impatient, George," Nancy advised with a grin. "We don't have proof that any of today's incidents is really cause for suspicion."

At this moment a foreign-make car went by. Nancy glanced casually at the driver, then gave a start. He was the man who had spoken to her on the train!

He slowed down and stared at the three girls and at the Fayne home. Nancy felt at once that he was memorizing the address. He gave a self-satisfied smile and drove on. Nancy noted his license number.

"I almost feel as if I'll hear from him again," she told herself, then revealed to the girls, who had not noticed the car's driver, that he was the man who had confronted her on the train.

"He's still interested in you," Bess teased.

But George found nothing to laugh about. "I don't like this, Nancy," she said seriously. "I remember he had a hard, calculating face."

Nancy, too, remained serious. A disturbing thought had suddenly occurred to her.

"Why," she told herself, "that man must have been trailing me. But I wonder for what reason?"

She determined, for the moment at least, not to mention her suspicions aloud and dropped the subject of the mysterious man. Presently she bade Bess and George good-by, climbed into her convertible, and drove home.

"I think I'll ask Dad what he thinks about that man Al's mysterious telephone message," Nancy decided as she hopped from the car.

She had often taken some of her puzzling problems to her father. He, in turn, frequently discussed his law cases with his daughter and found Nancy's suggestions practical.

"You look tired, dear," Carson Drew observed as she entered the living room and sank into a comfortable chair. "Have a big day shopping?"

"I can't remember when so much ever happened to me in one day." Nancy smiled despite her fatigue.

"I suppose I'll be getting the bills in a few days," her father remarked teasingly.

"It wasn't just the shopping, Dad," Nancy returned gravely.

Nancy now plunged into the story of the Oriental shop and the dropped perfume bottle, of her encounter with the stranger on the train, and the strange fact of having seen him a short while ago in a foreign-make car.

"What do you make of it?" she questioned.

Mr. Drew shrugged. "What did he look like?"

"The man seemed very polite, but he had a cruel look in his eyes." Nancy gave a brief description of him.

"Hm," Mr. Drew mused, "I can't say I like the sound of this."

"I wouldn't wonder about it," said Nancy, "except that the girl in the shop seemed so reluctant to sell the perfume. Why do you suppose she cared whether someone bought it?"

"Maybe she was instructed to save it for special customers," Mr. Drew suggested.

"Dad, you may have something there!" Nancy exclaimed.

She told her father about Joanne Byrd and described the office which they had visited together. She ended by showing him the figures which she had copied.

"This was almost all of the message," she explained. "I didn't have time to copy the rest. Can you figure it out?"

Carson Drew studied the sheet of paper. "I'm

not an expert on codes," he said finally, "but I suspect this might be one, since the man lied in saying these figures are market quotations."

"Can you decipher it?" Nancy asked eagerly.

"I wish I could, but it looks like a complicated one. It would probably take me days to figure out what these numbers stand for. Why don't you work on it yourself?"

"I don't know too much about codes," Nancy declared, "but perhaps I can learn!"

"I have a book you might use," her father offered. "It may not help much, since every code is different. Still, all codes have some features in common. For instance, in any language certain words are repeated more frequently than others. If you can figure out a frequency table, then look for certain numbers to appear more often than others, you may get somewhere."

"I'd like to try," Nancy said eagerly.

"This will be a good test for your sleuthing mind," her father said teasingly. "If you don't figure out the code, you can always turn this paper over to an expert."

"Not until I've had a fighting chance at it myself," Nancy answered with spirit.

"I'd really like to help you with this mystery," her father said, "but I'm so tied up with this Clifton case I just can't tackle anything else right now."

Immediately after dinner Mr. Drew retired to

his second-floor study to work on his law case. Nancy went to her bedroom to read the book on codes. When she finished, the girl detective took out the sheet on which she had copied the numbers and studied the figures intently.

"I'm sure the numbers stand for letters of the alphabet," Nancy told herself. "They must have been arranged in some pattern."

For over two hours Nancy tried combination after combination and applied it to the code. Nothing showed up until she hit upon the plan of four letters of the alphabet in sequence by number, the next four in reverse. Alternating in this manner and leaving two in the end bracket, Nancy scrutinized what she had worked out:

A	B	C	D	E	F	G	H	I	J	K	L	M
1	2	3	4	8	7	6	5	9	10	11	12	16

N	O	P	Q	R	S	T	U	V	W	X	Y	Z
15	14	13	17	18	19	20	24	23	22	21	25	26

"I've hit it!" she thought excitedly.

CHAPTER IV

A Switch in Jobs

1653 112   129 156͠2 16   882 091 56̲18̲
 C a l   li ng m ee ti ng͠

The numbers with the marks above or below them stymied Nancy completely. Most of the others fell neatly into place and spelled:

"Calling meeting," Nancy repeated. "But where? And by whom?" She yawned, weary from her long concentration. "My brain's too fogged to figure out anything more," she told herself. "I'll tackle this another time."

The next morning Nancy and her father enjoyed a leisurely breakfast. He praised her for hitting upon the key to the code but agreed that solving the rest of it would be difficult.

"Keep at it," he advised, smiling fondly at his daughter. "By the way, I won't be home to lunch or dinner today because of this Clifton case."

"I thought I'd visit Joanne and try to cheer her up," Nancy said. "Do you, by any chance, know anyone who's looking for an office girl?" she added.

Mr. Drew shook his head. "No. I'm afraid I don't. But if I hear of anything I'll let you know."

"I feel that Joanne isn't the type to be in the hectic business world," Nancy remarked. "If it weren't that she wants to help her grandmother, I doubt that she'd even try for a city position."

After Carson Drew had left for his office, Nancy busied herself around the house, helping Hannah. When the housework was finally done, Nancy settled herself in an easy chair and delved into the code book once more. But she found no new hints to help break her own set of numbers.

Nancy, Bess, and George had planned to start for Riverside Heights early in the afternoon, so as soon as the luncheon dishes had been cleared away, Nancy was off to pick up the other girls. By two-thirty they had reached Joanne's rooming house.

The landlady answered Nancy's knock on the front door and informed her that Joanne had left two hours before to see about a job. She would be back at three o'clock. The woman invited the girls in, but the living room looked so dark and dreary that they preferred to wait outside in the car.

"It's too bad Joanne has to stay in a dismal

place like that," Nancy remarked, "especially when she's accustomed to farm life."

"I sure hope she finds something," Bess added. "Maybe luck will be with her today."

Within fifteen minutes the girls spotted Joanne at a distance. She did not notice the car, and unaware that she was being observed, walked slowly toward the rooming house, her head drooping dejectedly.

"She didn't get the job," George murmured. "I feel so sorry for her."

As Joanne approached, Nancy called to her. Joanne glanced up quickly and mustered a smile.

"No luck today?" Bess questioned.

"None at all," Joanne answered with a sigh. She came over to the car and stood leaning against the door. "I tried half a dozen places, but I couldn't land a thing. I'll just have to try again tomorrow."

In the face of such spirit on Joanne's part, the girls could do nothing but encourage her, though secretly they feared she would have no better luck the next day.

"How about coming for a short ride?" Nancy invited.

"I'd love it," Joanne accepted eagerly. "It's so hot and stuffy in my room—" She hesitated, then added, "Of course, I guess it is everywhere these days!"

Nancy took a road that led out of the city and soon they were driving past cultivated fields of corn and wheat. Gradually, Joanne became more cheerful.

"It's so good to be out in the country again!" she declared, gazing wistfully toward a farmhouse nestled in the rolling hills. "That place looks something like Red Gate Farm, only not half so attractive. I wish you all could visit me there sometime!"

"So do we!" Nancy said enthusiastically. "Wouldn't it be wonderful to hike over hills and breathe in the fresh clean air?"

"I've always wanted to spend a vacation on a farm," Bess declared longingly. "Just imagine having cream an inch thick!"

"Just what you need for reducing!" her cousin teased her.

"You wouldn't have to worry about that." Joanne smiled. "We keep only one cow."

When the girls later left Joanne at the door of her boardinghouse, they had the satisfaction of knowing she was in a more cheerful frame of mind.

"We'll keep in touch with you, Joanne," Nancy promised as they said good-by.

"I have a feeling we'll be seeing a lot more of each other," Joanne called after them. "So please do call me Jo! I'd much prefer it."

"Jo it is!" they agreed merrily. "Good-by for now."

Nancy and her friends had just started back to River Heights when Nancy checked her gas gauge and decided to stop at a filling station. The girls were idly watching passers-by when suddenly a young woman, walking with mincing steps because of her extremely high heels, attracted Nancy's attention. Nancy gasped in recognition.

There was no mistaking the distinctive Oriental features. The clerk in the perfume shop!

Nancy turned to her companions. "Look at that girl who just crossed over. Isn't she the same one who sold you the perfume, Bess?"

"You mean the one who tried *not* to sell me the perfume, don't you?" Bess joked. "Yes, she's the same girl!"

Their eyes followed the girl up the street. She had not glanced toward them, but had passed the filling station and continued on.

"Now, what can she be doing here?" Nancy wondered. She got out of the car and stood watching the girl, who entered an office building a short distance farther up the street.

"That's funny," Nancy said to her friends, who were peering from the car windows. "I think that's the very place where Jo applied for a position!"

"You don't suppose that perfume girl has two jobs, do you?" George questioned.

"I'd sure like to find out," the young detective answered.

Just then the attendant approached. Nancy paid him and stepped back into the car.

"We must try to follow her," she declared, starting the motor. They pulled up near the office building into which the young woman had disappeared.

"You two wait here and keep watch," Nancy said. "If I'm not back in a few minutes, you'd better come and see what's going on."

"Aye, aye, sir!" George said mockingly. "We're at your service! But be careful!"

Nancy alighted, hurried up the street, and went into the building. The halls were deserted. Evidently the girl had gone into one of the offices. But which one? As Nancy stood uncertainly staring up and down, she spotted a handyman coming down the corridor.

"Did you see a girl come into the building just a moment ago?" she inquired.

"Oriental?" the man demanded, resting on his broom.

Nancy nodded eagerly. "Yes, she looks rather Oriental."

"Oh, you mean Yvonne Wong."

"Do you know her?" Nancy said, thinking that with the name Yvonne, the girl was probably part French.

"No, but I heard that man she works for, with

the loud voice and the swell clothes, call her by
that name."

"She works here?" Nancy inquired in surprise.

"Guess so. She must be a new girl. Came here
yesterday."

"I see," Nancy murmured, thinking Yvonne
Wong had managed a rather sudden change of
jobs. "Could you tell me in which office she
works?"

Her questions evidently had begun to annoy
the handyman. "In 305. If you're so interested,"
he said brusquely, "why don't you go in and ask
her what you want to know?"

"Thank you," Nancy responded with a polite smile, turning away. "I won't trouble you any
further."

Nancy had taken only a few steps when she
thought of one more question and came back. "By
the way," she said in a casual tone, "what sort of
office is 305?"

The man regarded her suspiciously. "How
should I know?" he demanded bluntly. "They
don't pay me to go stickin' my nose in other folks'
business. I got my own work."

Nancy could see that she was not going to learn
any more from the man, so she left the building
and joined Bess and George, who were waiting
anxiously at the door.

"Well, what did you manage to find out?" Bess

queried, as the three girls walked toward the car.

"Quite a bit," Nancy answered meditatively. She was certain that she could not have been mistaken. Yvonne Wong was the same girl who only yesterday had waited on them in the Oriental shop. Why had she changed positions?

"Well," George broke into her thoughts, "don't keep us in suspense!"

Nancy answered all their questions as she drove toward River Heights, explaining that the young woman's name was Yvonne Wong and that she was a new girl in the office—the same office Nancy and Joanne had visited.

"But what about Yvonne's job at the Oriental perfume shop?" asked George.

"I don't know," Nancy admitted, "and the handyman wouldn't give me any indication as to the type of business it was!"

Nancy recalled the strange telephone call which had been made while she and Joanne were in the office. She distinctly remembered that some mention had been made of a girl who had been found for the position, and that the man who called himself "Al" had said that one "couldn't be too careful."

"I wouldn't be so suspicious about Yvonne," Nancy added, "except I have a feeling she didn't get that job by chance. She must have been chosen because she was especially suited to the situation—whatever that is."

"There's something underhanded about the whole thing, but we haven't much to go on," Bess declared.

Nancy agreed. "Some clue may turn up. Anyway, we have Jo to think about for the time being."

It was getting dark as Nancy dropped off Bess and then George at their homes.

It rained so hard the following day that Nancy stayed indoors and tried to figure out the remaining symbols of the code. Using the same alphabetical key, 16 was M, $\overline{5}$ equaled H, $\widetilde{2}$ could be B, and $\underline{18}$ stood for R.

"MHBR," Nancy pondered. "That doesn't make any sense. Perhaps those marks over and under the letters are a second code," she reasoned. "If only I could decipher *them*, I might know who's calling what meeting, and where."

The next morning a bright sun shone. While Nancy was busy with chores around the house, the phone rang and she went to answer it.

"Hello, Nancy," said a quiet voice. "This is Jo. How are you?"

"Oh, Jo, I'm fine," Nancy replied eagerly. "Did you find a job?" she asked hopefully.

"Not yet," Joanne answered sadly. "But I have some other news."

"I hope it's good," Nancy said.

"I just talked with my grandmother on the phone. I must go home right away. She told me that soon after I left, a man called and made an offer to buy Red Gate. His price was so low, she didn't accept. He was very persistent, though, and gave her five days to think it over."

"Yes?" Nancy prompted.

"Well," the other girl went on, "in the meantime, Grandmother decided to try raising money by taking in boarders. She placed an ad in the paper that same day."

"Good for her!" Nancy exclaimed. "Has she had any replies?"

"No," Joanne said worriedly. "Even though the ad hasn't run very long, Gram's discouraged. I'm afraid she has changed her mind and intends to take that man's offer. She said he's coming to Red Gate tomorrow at five o'clock and bringing papers for her to sign."

There was a pause, then Joanne burst out, "Nancy, I just can't let Gram go through with this, and if I'm not there, she'll accept the man's offer. She mustn't give up Red Gate Farm yet! That's why I must get home and persuade her not to sell."

"By all means," Nancy agreed. "I suppose you'll take the train to Round Valley in the morning?"

"That's the horrible part, Nancy," Joanne said dejectedly. "I'll have only enough money for train fare half the way after I pay my room rent."

"No need to do that, Jo," Nancy said eagerly. "You get your bag packed and be ready to leave at ten o'clock tomorrow morning!"

CHAPTER V

Money, Money!

As NANCY reflected on her plan, another idea occurred to her. She was sure that Bess and George would love the chance to spend a vacation on a farm, since they had both mentioned it the other day. Nancy did some mental arithmetic and came to the conclusion that three steady boarders who paid their bills regularly might help to lessen the amount of the mortgage interest payments that threatened Red Gate.

"And also keep Mrs. Byrd from selling the place," Nancy thought. "I hope Dad agrees to my making the trip."

That evening at dinner Mr. Drew said, "I'll be out of town for a week or so, Nancy. Do you think you can get some of your friends to stay with you?"

"I have an even better idea," Nancy replied, and smiled.

She outlined her plan to help Joanne Byrd. Her father consented enthusiastically, proud as always of Nancy's desire to assist others.

It was not so easy to convince Bess and George, when Nancy telephoned them. They both wanted to help Joanne and agreed that a week or two in the country would be very pleasant, but there were complications. If George went, it meant she would lose out on a camping trip. Bess had planned to visit an aunt in Chicago, but admitted that the trip could be postponed.

"There's one thing about it," George said laughingly as she finally agreed to give up the camping trip. "I've never been with you yet that we didn't run into an adventure or mystery! Maybe a trip to Red Gate will be exciting."

Bess and George had no trouble in getting their parents' consent. It was decided that Nancy would pick up Joanne first, then come back for the cousins, since River Heights was on the way to Round Valley.

Nancy packed her clothes that night after telephoning the plans to Joanne. As she was closing the suitcase, her eyes fell upon the copy of the coded message which lay on the dressing table.

"I'd better take it along and work on it whenever I have the chance," she decided.

Nancy got up early the next morning and had breakfast with her father. After exchanging fond good-bys with him and Hannah, she hurried to her car.

It was close to ten o'clock when Nancy reached Riverside Heights. She stopped at a downtown service station and had her convertible filled with gas and checked for oil. Then she drove to Joanne's boardinghouse.

Her passenger was waiting. Nancy was glad to find that Joanne seemed to be in better spirits.

"It'll be such fun, all of us going together," Joanne said, "and I know Gram will be happy to have you stay as long as you like."

"Only on the condition that we are paying guests," Nancy insisted.

"We'll see about that later," Joanne said, smiling.

They put her suitcase into the trunk of the car and soon were on their way back to River Heights. Assured by Joanne that they would be welcome at Red Gate, the cousins brought out their suitcases and put them in the luggage compartment.

George took Nancy aside and said excitedly, "A little while ago a man phoned here and asked for Miss Fayne. When I answered, he said, 'Listen, miss, tell that snoopy friend of yours to *stop* her snooping, or she'll be sorry!' Then he hung up without giving his name."

Nancy set her jaw, then smiled. "Whoever he

is, he has a guilty conscience. So my suspicions were well founded."

"Who *do* you think he is?" George asked.

"Either the strange man on the train who followed me here, or some accomplice of his."

"I'm glad for your sake we're going away, Nancy," stated George.

"Let's not say anything about this to Jo," Nancy advised, as she and George walked back to the car.

"It's a perfect day for our trip to the country," Joanne said excitedly.

George could see by the expression on Joanne's face that a visit to Red Gate Farm with her new friends was far more important to her than any other plans the girls might have had.

"I agree one hundred per cent!" George answered happily as she stepped into the car.

"And I'll be so glad to get out of this heat," Bess chimed in with a sigh. "I spent practically the whole night dreaming about the cool, refreshing breezes in the country."

As Nancy steered the convertible in the direction of Round Valley, she said with an eager smile, "We're off to rescue Red Gate Farm!"

Nancy and her friends thoroughly enjoyed the scenic route to Round Valley. They stopped for a quick lunch and then continued their drive. The winding roads led through cool groves and skirted sparkling little lakes. Each hilltop brought a different and beautiful view.

Gradually the worried expression completely left Joanne's eyes, and color came into her thin face. She began to laugh heartily at the antics of Bess and George. As they rode along she told the girls a great deal about her home.

"You'll like Red Gate, I'm sure," she said enthusiastically. "We haven't any riding horses, but there will be plenty of other things to do. We can explore the cave, for one thing."

"Cave?" Bess questioned with interest. "How exciting! What kind is it? A home for bears or a pirate's den?"

Joanne laughed. "There's a large cavern located on the farm. No one knows how it came to be there, but we think it must have been made a long time ago by an underground river."

"You must have explored it before this!" Nancy exclaimed.

"Oh, yes, of course, though I'll admit I never did very thoroughly, and I haven't been near the cave for years. As a child I was always afraid of the place—it looked so dark and gloomy. Lately I've been too busy working around the farm."

"We'll have to put that at the top of our list!" George declared. "I love spooky things."

"Well, I'm not so sure I do," Bess admitted.

Nancy laughed. "We may even find hidden treasure in the walls."

"I wish you could." Joanne sighed. "It certainly would come in handy."

The hours passed quickly as the travelers alternately sang and chatted. "Why, it's almost four o'clock!" George announced in surprise.

"We've made good time," Nancy remarked.

Bess spoke up plaintively. "I'm half-starved. It's been *ages* since lunch. I could go for a gooey sundae."

The others laughed, but agreed they were hungry too.

"Let's watch for a roadside stand," Nancy proposed. "I'll have to stop soon for gas, anyway."

"We'll come to one soon," Joanne spoke up. "We're in Round Valley now."

A few minutes later she pointed out a combination filling station and lunchroom which looked clean and inviting. Nancy turned the convertible into the driveway and parked out of the way of other drivers who might want to stop for gasoline.

The group entered the lunchroom and took seats at one of the small white tables. They all decided on chocolate nut sundaes topped with whipped cream.

"Here goes another pound." Bess sighed as she gave her order. "But I'd rather be pleasantly plump than give up sundaes!"

Though there were few customers in the room, the woman in charge, who also did the serving, was extremely slow in filling the orders. Twice Nancy glanced at her watch.

"If you'll excuse me," she said, "I'll step outside and get the gasoline. It will save us a little time in getting started. Don't wait for me if our sundaes come."

She drove the car over to the pump and asked the attendant to fill the tank. Before he could do so, however, a large, high-powered sedan pulled up to the other pump, coming to an abrupt stop almost parallel to Nancy's car.

"Give me five and make it snappy!" a voice called out impatiently.

The attendant glanced inquiringly at Nancy Drew. "Do you mind?" he asked.

"Wait on them first if you like," she said graciously.

Nancy observed the passengers with interest. There were three rather coarse-looking men, accompanied by a woman.

Nancy could not see the face of the driver, for it was turned away from her. But suddenly he opened the door of his car.

"I'm goin' inside and get a couple bottles of ginger ale," she heard him grumble to his companions.

As he stepped from the automobile and turned, Nancy saw his face. He was the mysterious man who had spoken to her that day on the train!

In view of the telephone call George had received, Nancy did not wish to be observed. She turned her head quickly, leaned down, and pretended to be studying a road map. "I hope he doesn't recognize me!" Nancy thought, "or see my license plate!"

To her relief, the man walked in front of the convertible without a sideward glance. At that moment the woman alighted and walked toward the lunchroom, passing close to Nancy's car. She was tall and slender, with blond hair that was almost shoulder length. Nancy's attention was suddenly arrested when she detected on the stranger a familiar scent—Blue Jade perfume!

After the driver and the blond woman had entered the lunchroom, Nancy gazed at the two men who remained in the automobile. They were the sort Carson Drew would describe as "tough customers."

The blond woman soon reappeared and got back into the sedan. Then the driver came out carrying the cold drinks. Without looking in Nancy's direction, he addressed the attendant harshly.

"Say, ain't you finished yet?"

He turned to one of the men in the car and handed him the bottles of ginger ale.

"Hold these, will you, Hank? I got to pay this bird!"

Nancy started. "That man in Room 305 called one of his friends 'Hank' over the telephone," she said to herself. "Could he be this person?"

Her attention was drawn back to the driver, who was paying the attendant. He took a thick roll of bills from his pocket, and with a careless gesture peeled off a ten-dollar bill.

"Aren't you afraid to carry such a wad around, sir?" the attendant questioned, gazing admiringly at the thick roll.

The driver laughed boisterously. "Plenty more where this comes from. Eh, Hank?"

"You bet! My roll makes his look like a flat tire! Just feast your eyes on this!" He flashed an even larger roll of bills in the amazed attendant's face.

The filling-station man shrugged. "I'll have to go inside to get your change."

The moment he had disappeared, the third man in the car muttered to his companions, "You fools! Do you want to make him suspicious? Pipe down!" He spoke in a low tone but the wind carried his voice in Nancy's direction.

"Maurice is right," the driver admitted. "The fellow is only a cornball, but we can't be too careful."

The attendant returned with the change. The driver pocketed it and drove off without another word. Nancy instinctively noted the license number of the car. On impulse she went to a

phone booth and dialed her friend Chief Mc-
Ginnis of the River Heights Police Department.

"I'll ask him to let me know who owns both the
sedan and the foreign-make car that slowed down
at George's house," she determined. "Then I'll
find out about the driver, the woman wearing the
Blue Jade, the men named Maurice and Hank,
and maybe the man in Room 305!"

CHAPTER VI

A Worrisome Journey

"Some class, eh?" the attendant remarked to Nancy as she came back to her car. "Must be millionaires."

"Or racketeers," Nancy thought. As soon as her gas tank was filled, she paid the bill and hurried back into the lunchroom. The girls already had been served.

"What took you so long?" Bess asked.

"Another car drove up and I had to wait," Nancy answered simply. She sat down, thoughtfully eating her sundae.

"What's the matter with you?" George demanded presently. "You've hardly said a word since you sat down."

Nancy looked around and saw that no one was seated near their table. In whispers she told what had happened.

"Oh, dear," said Bess, "maybe that man on the

train found out where we're going and is on his way there too!"

"Don't be silly," George chided her cousin. "If he's in some shady deal around River Heights, he'd be glad to have our young sleuth out of the way."

Joanne looked a bit worried, but all she said was, "I think we'd better be on our way. I *have* to be there before that man comes to buy the farm. I must talk Gram out of it!"

The girls finished the sundaes and picked up their checks, but Nancy insisted upon paying.

"I want to break this twenty-dollar bill Dad gave me," she said. "I've spent most of my smaller bills."

The waitress changed the bill for her without comment and the girls left the lunchroom. As they climbed into the car, Nancy glanced anxiously at the sky. There was a dark overcast in the west.

"It does look like rain over my way," Joanne observed. "And we leave the paved road and take a dirt one about five miles from the farm."

"I'm afraid it's going to be a race against time," Nancy warned, starting the car. "A bad storm on a dirt road won't help matters at all!"

The girls now noticed a change in the countryside. The hills had become steeper and the valleys deeper. The farms dotting the landscape were very attractive.

Nancy made fast time, for she was bent on beating the storm. The sky became gloomier and overcast. Soon the first raindrops appeared on the windshield. "We're in for a downpour all right!" Nancy declared grimly, as she turned onto the dirt road.

Soon there was thunder and lightning, and the rain came down in torrents.

"Listen to that wind!" Bess exclaimed. "It's enough to blow us off the road!"

The next minute everyone groaned in dismay, and Nancy braked the car. Across the road stood a wooden blockade. On it was a sign:

Detour
Bridge Under Repair

George read it aloud in disgust. An arrow on the sign indicated a narrow road to the right. As Nancy made the turn, Joanne gave a sigh.

"Oh, dear," she said, "this back way will take us much longer to reach Red Gate."

The detour led through a woodland of tall trees. Daylight had been blotted out entirely, and even with the car's headlights on full, Nancy could barely see ahead. Again she was forced to slow down.

Suddenly a jagged streak of lightning hit a big oak a short distance from the car. It splintered the tree.

"Oh!" screamed Bess. "This is terrible!"

Nancy pretended to be calm, but she really was very much worried. She decided it would be safer to get away from the dangerous line of trees, any one of which might crash down on them!

"How long is this stretch of woods?" she asked Joanne.

"Oh, perhaps five hundred feet."

"We'll have to chance it." Nancy drove as quickly as she dared in the darkness. The girls breathed sighs of relief when open country was reached.

But Joanne's fears were not yet over. "Watch out!" she advised. "There's a sharp, treacherous curve very soon, just before we take the turnoff for the farm."

By now the brief storm had moved off to a distant sky and it was easier to see the boundaries of the slippery road. Nancy rounded a curve, but as the car took the turn, the wheels on the right side sank into the thick mud of a ditch, bringing the car to a lurching halt.

The unexpected mishap stunned the girls for a moment. Finally Bess found her voice. "Now what?"

Nancy endeavored to drive the car out of the ditch, but it was useless. "Well"—she sighed—"we may as well jump out and examine the car. Keep your fingers crossed."

They found the convertible at a lopsided angle. The right wheels, however, were firmly anchored by the mud. The four girls attempted to push the car, but without success.

"I'll look in the trunk," Nancy said, "to see if there's something to help us."

Nancy found two pieces of heavy burlap. Bess and George put them in front of the two back wheels for traction. Then they gathered and broke up some brush to make a mat for each tire.

"I hope this works," Joanne said, taking her place to assist in pushing the car. "There probably won't be anyone else using this desolate road who could help us. "I— I'm afraid we won't reach the farm in time!"

Nancy stepped into the car and started the motor, easing the gas and slowly rocking the convertible back and forth. Inch by inch the tires crept forward, finally catching on the burlap and brush and rolling out of the ditch.

"We've done it!" Bess shouted proudly.

"With a little outside help!" George panted with a grin. The girls laughed from sheer relief.

They started off again, more slowly than before. But they had gone only a mile when a new storm seemed to be coming up. In less than five minutes complete darkness descended again, bringing another deluge of rain. Deafening thunderclaps instantly followed vivid forks of lightning.

Of necessity, Nancy once more kept the automobile at a snail's pace. It was impossible to see more than a few feet ahead. Anxiously Joanne kept glancing at her watch. "It's five-fifteen," she announced nervously.

Nancy tried to assuage the worried girl's fears. "This storm may have delayed your grandmother's caller."

The wind and rain continued unabated. As the convertible climbed the brow of a hill, there was a brilliant flash of lightning. George, who was seated in front with Nancy, screamed, "Don't hit her!"

Nancy jammed on the brakes so quickly that the rear of the car skidded around sideways in the road.

"Who?" she demanded, horrified.

"The woman in the road! Didn't you see her? Maybe she's under the car!"

Heartsick, Nancy jumped out one door, Bess another. They peered under the car, alongside it, in back of it. They could see no one.

"Are you sure you saw a woman?" Nancy inquired.

Just then another streak of lightning illuminated the sky, and Bess called out, "There goes someone running across that field!"

Nancy glanced quickly in that direction and saw the running figure of a woman. At that same moment the woman looked back over her shoulder, revealing a thin, haggard face. Nancy judged her to be in her early fifties.

All four girls stared in mystification. Nancy and Bess returned to the car and the journey was resumed.

"Why would any sane person be walking in such a storm?" Bess spoke up finally.

"She's headed in the direction of the cavern," said Joanne, and explained that they were now nearing the farm. "Maybe she's one of those strange people over there!"

Nancy and her friends were immediately curious. Before they could ask what Joanne meant, the car reached the crest of a steep hill and Joanne cried out:

"There's Red Gate Farm!" She pointed to the valley below them.

The storm had let up and the sun was coming out. The River Heights girls could clearly see the forty-acre farm, with its groves of pine trees and a winding river which curled along the valley. Everything looked green and fresh after the heavy rain.

"It's beautiful!" exclaimed Bess.

"And cool—and peaceful," Joanne added excitedly.

"Don't count on much relaxation with Nancy around," George advised their new friend. "She'll find some adventure to occupy every waking hour!"

"Yes," Bess agreed. "Adventure with mystery added."

Nancy smiled. She reflected on the two mysteries she had already encountered; the unsolved case of the Blue Jade perfume and the strange code.

As the car descended into the valley, the girls caught a better glimpse of the farm with its huge red barn and various adjoining sheds and the large, rambling house, partly covered with vines. There were bright-red geraniums in the window boxes, and a freshly painted picket fence surrounding the yard.

Nancy stopped the car in front of the big red gate which opened into the garden. "Oh, I hope it's not too late!" Joanne cried as she sprang out to unlatch the gate.

CHAPTER VII

Nature Cult

NANCY drove in to Red Gate Farm and parked. She consulted her watch and noted with dismay it was quarter to six. By now the farmhouse door had opened, and a gray-haired woman in a crisp gingham dress and white apron came hurrying out to meet them. Her blue eyes were bright as she welcomed Joanne warmly.

"My granddaughter told me how kind you all were to her in the city," she said to Nancy and her friends. "I can't thank you enough."

"Gram!" Joanne exclaimed. "I can't stand the suspense. Did you sell the farm to that man?"

Mrs. Byrd shook her head. "Mercy! I was so excited at your coming back I forgot to tell you. He phoned a little while ago and said that because of the storm he'd rather come here tomorrow—he could wait one more day."

Not only Joanne, but her visitors, heaved sighs

of relief. Further discussion of the subject was deferred when Mrs. Byrd insisted the girls freshen up for supper.

They entered the large, rambling house, and a little later everyone sat down in the plainly furnished but comfortable dining room. Mrs. Byrd appeared very happy as she bustled about, serving the delicious meal of hot biscuits, sizzling ham, sweet potatoes, and coffee. The girls had not realized how hungry they were.

"Nothing like driving through a storm to work up an appetite." George grinned.

It was not until dessert—freshly baked lemon meringue pie—that Joanne mentioned again what was uppermost in her mind. "Gram," she said gently, "*please* call up that man and tell him you don't want to sell our farm. *Please*. We'll find a way to stay here, somehow. I'm sure there'll be answers to your ads for boarders."

Nancy quickly spoke up. "Yes, Mrs. Byrd. It certainly would be a shame to give up Red Gate. And besides, George, Bess, and I would like to be paying guests for a while—if you'd like us to stay, that is."

"Of course I want you all here as long as possible. But I really can't accept any money," Mrs. Byrd protested. "You have been so wonderful to Jo."

"If you won't let us pay our share, we'll have to return home tomorrow," Nancy insisted.

Mrs. Byrd finally relented and declared with a smile: "I believe I was just waiting to be dissuaded from taking that Mr. Kent's offer. I'll call him right now. He gave me his telephone number."

The girls followed her into the kitchen, and sat down while Mrs. Byrd went to the phone there and put in the call.

"Mr. Kent? I've decided not to sell Red Gate Farm—at any price. . . . No. I . . . No. . . . Absolutely." The woman winced and held the phone away from her ear.

Nancy and her friends exchanged glances. The man was evidently incensed and was speaking so loudly they could hear his voice easily. Finally Mrs. Byrd put down the receiver.

"Well, I'm glad that man isn't going to own Red Gate," she declared. "He certainly was unpleasant. He even said I might regret my decision."

Joanne's face was radiant and she hugged her grandmother. "I feel so much better now." She turned to her new friends. "Somehow, I know you're going to bring us luck, Nancy, Bess, and George."

Suddenly Mrs. Byrd said, "Goodness! I've forgotten to look in our mailbox today."

"I'll go." Joanne hurried outside and was back in a minute, several envelopes in her hand.

"Gram! One of these is from the Round Valley *Gazette*. Do you think—?" Excitedly she handed the mail to her grandmother.

The girls watched eagerly as Mrs. Byrd tore open a long, bulky envelope and took out a number of enclosed letters. She looked at them quickly. A smile spread over her face.

"Gram, are they answers to the ad for boarders?" Joanne asked excitedly.

Mrs. Byrd nodded. "I can hardly believe it! Two people are arriving the day after tomorrow. First, a Mrs. Salisbury, then a Mr. Abbott. Several others will come later this month."

"Wonderful!" Nancy said, and immediately offered her assistance in getting rooms ready.

"Count Bess and me in too," said George.

Joanne and her grandmother at first demurred, but were outvoted. "Very well." Mrs. Byrd smiled. "Tomorrow afternoon will be time enough to get things ready."

Later, as the guests bid her good night, Mrs. Byrd said:

"Jo was right. You three girls *have* brought us luck. Bless you!"

George and Bess were shown to the room in which they would sleep. Nancy was to share Joanne's bedroom.

"Oh, how sweet it smells in here," Joanne commented, as Nancy unpacked.

"That's some of the Oriental perfume which splashed on my clothes in the train," said Nancy. "It certainly is strong and lasting!"

When Nancy awoke the next morning, warm sunlight was streaming through the windows. Joanne had already gone downstairs. Nancy's first thought was to phone Police Chief McGinnis and find out about the owner, or owners, of the cars driven by the suspicious man. After dressing hurriedly she went to the first floor and placed the call.

"Good morning, Nancy," the officer said. "Here's the information you wanted. Both cars were rented from drive-yourself agencies by a man named Philip Smith, a native of Dallas, Texas. They've been returned."

Nancy thanked the chief and hung up. "That clue wasn't any help," she thought. "None of those suspicious men talked like a Texan. The name Philip Smith was probably phony, and made up on the spur of the moment. Also, a forged driver's license might have been used."

Presently Bess and George came down and the girls enjoyed a delicious breakfast of pancakes and sausages. Afterward, Joanne took the girls on a tour of the farm. She showed them the lovely gardens, a large chicken house, and her pet goat, Chester.

A turkey took a dislike to Bess and chased her to the farmhouse porch, much to the amusement of the onlookers! Joanne came to the rescue and chased the turkey away.

"Our farm isn't very well stocked," she admitted as she led the way to the barn. "We keep only one cow and one work horse. Poor old Michael should be retired on a pension, but we can't afford to lose him yet!"

Joanne cheerfully hailed the hired man. Reuben Ames was about forty years old, red-haired, and rather quiet in manner. He acknowledged each introduction with a mumbled "Pleased to meet you, miss," and extended a work-worn hand for each girl to shake. Reuben shifted uncomfortably and then returned to the barn.

"Reuben is as good as gold, even if he is bashful," Joanne told the girls. "I don't know what we'd do without him."

"We'd better keep an eye on Bess," George teased. "She'll be breaking another heart."

Bess made a good-natured retort as the girls started for the orchard. George demonstrated her agility by climbing the nearest apple tree. Once back at the farmhouse, Nancy asked curiously, "Jo, please tell us more about the cave that you spoke about yesterday. I'm bursting to know all about it."

"Well, the cave is on a piece of land along the river which Gram rents out."

"Oh, then I suppose it'll be impossible for us to visit the cavern," Nancy commented.

"I don't see why we can't. It's still our land."
Joanne frowned. "A queer lot of people are rent-
ing it, though."

"How do you mean?" Nancy questioned, re-
calling Joanne's remark of the previous day.

"They're some sort of sect—a nature cult, I
think, and part of a large organization. At least
that's what it said in the letter Gram received
from their leader. Anyway, this group calls itself
the Black Snake Colony."

"Pleasant name," Bess observed cynically.

"I'm not sure what they do," Joanne admitted.
"We've never even spoken to any members. I
suppose they believe in living an outdoor life."

"You can live that way without joining a nature cult," George said dryly. "I suppose they
dance when the dew is on the grass and such nonsense!"

"Believe it or not they *do* dance!" Joanne
laughed. "But only nights when the moon is out.
I've seen them from here in the moonlight. It's
an eerie sight. They wear white robes and flit
around waving their arms. They even wear
masks!"

"Masks!" Nancy exclaimed. "Why?"

"I can't imagine. It all sounds senseless. But
the rent money is helpful."

"Do they live in this cavern?" George asked in
amazement.

"No, they live in shacks and tents near the

river. I've never really had the nerve to visit the place. Of course if you girls went along—"

"When can we go?" Nancy asked excitedly.

"I'll speak to Gram," Joanne offered.

"It's odd you've never spoken to any of the colony members," Nancy remarked thoughtfully. "Who pays the rent?"

"It's sent by mail. They even leased the land that way."

"Didn't it strike you as a peculiar way of doing business?" Nancy asked.

"Yes," Joanne admitted, "but I suppose it's part of their creed, or whatever you call it. They probably don't believe in mingling with people outside the cult. That's often the case."

Directly after lunch the girls helped the Byrds straighten and clean the rooms for the expected boarders. They hung curtains, newly made by Mrs. Byrd, and put fresh flowers in each room.

At the end of the afternoon they were very pleased with the result.

"All you girls have worked hard enough," Mrs. Byrd said. "You go rest while I fix supper."

She was insistent, so Joanne led her friends to the porch. Bess stretched out in the hammock and picked up the day's newspaper. The others chatted. Suddenly Bess gave an exclamation of surprise.

"Nancy," she asked tensely, "what was the name of that girl who sold me the perfume?"

"Wong," Nancy answered in amazement. "Yvonne Wong. Why?"

"Because there's an article in the paper that mentions her name!" Bess thrust the newspaper into Nancy's hands, indicating the paragraph. "Wow! This is something! Read it yourself!"

CHAPTER VIII

Hillside Ghosts

NANCY read aloud:

" 'The Hale Syndicate, which has been engaged in the illegal importation of Oriental articles, has been dissolved by court order.' " Nancy looked up and said, "I don't see what that has to do with our perfume friend Yvonne Wong."

"A great deal," Bess declared. "Read on and you'll find out!"

"Oh!" Nancy exclaimed a few seconds later. "Yvonne was employed by the syndicate as a clerk in their shop. She hasn't been indicted, because of insufficient evidence, and the top men have skipped!"

Bess nodded, realizing the impact of her important discovery. "That perfume store we visited must have been owned by the syndicate!"

"How long ago was the fraud discovered?" George asked.

"The article doesn't say," Nancy returned. "It has just now been made public."

"It doesn't surprise me that the Wong girl was mixed up in some underhanded affair," George remarked. "I didn't like her attitude from the beginning!"

"Nor did I," Bess added. "And I liked her less after Nancy found out she had received the job Jo wanted."

"I'm certainly glad I *didn't* get that job." Joanne smiled. "I'd much rather be here."

"Do you suppose Yvonne knew the work of the syndicate was dishonest?" Bess asked with concern.

"I'm sure of it," George answered flatly. "But it looks as if she and the others slipped out quickly when the federal authorities became aware of the racket."

All this time Nancy had been staring into space. It had occurred to her that Yvonne Wong might still be employed by the syndicate. Undoubtedly the name and offices had been changed to throw off the federal authorities. Was Room 305 now the syndicate's headquarters?

Nancy immediately thought of the coded message she had brought with her. "The third number in it, 5, was the letter H," she told herself. Then she reflected on the recent newspaper article about the syndicate.

"This 'H' might stand for Hale!" she thought

excitedly. "And the line over it might mean that someone by this name is important—the ringleader, perhaps! I must talk to Chief McGinnis again. I may have stumbled onto a clue to those missing Hale Syndicate men!"

After supper she phoned the chief and propounded her theory. "Well, Nancy," he said, "it sounds as if you might have picked up a clue, sure enough. Send me a copy of that code and I'll get busy on it."

After Nancy completed the call, she and the other girls studied the code once more.

Gazing at the 16 and the 5, Nancy suddenly said, "M—M—why that *could* stand for Maurice! Maybe that man's name is Maurice Hale!"

"Now I'll sleep better," Bess sighed. The girls went to bed happy and excited.

The next day everyone's attention was focused on a new boarder. Shortly after church services, Mrs. Alice Salisbury and her daughter Nona arrived in an expensive sedan. Mrs. Salisbury walked with a cane, and complained loudly of her arthritis as the girls helped her into the house.

Nona waited only long enough to see that her mother was made comfortable. Then she announced that she must hurry back to the city nearby, where she lived.

"Mother was born on a farm," she told Mrs. Byrd as she stepped into the car, "and she simply pines for the country. I thought this arrangement might be ideal since she's never entirely happy with me in the city. I'll drive down to see her week ends. I do hope she'll be happier here at Red Gate Farm."

Joanne and her friends hoped so too, but they were not at all certain, for it became increasingly apparent that Mrs. Salisbury could not be happy anywhere. She found no fault with the immaculate farmhouse or the lovely view from her bedroom window, but she constantly complained of her various aches and pains. She talked incessantly about her many operations. She had a sharp tongue and delighted in using it.

"She wouldn't be so bad, if only she'd stop talking operations," George burst out. "Makes me feel as though I'm ready for the hospital myself!"

By the time the girls had adjusted themselves to Mrs. Salisbury, the second boarder arrived. He was Karl Abbott, a diamond-in-the-rough type of man. In spite of his sixty-three years, he boasted that he was as spry as his son Karl Jr., who had brought him.

Karl Jr., who worked in a nearby city, was a personable young man. The girls, particularly Bess, were sorry he could not remain with his father.

The girls liked Mr. Abbott very much, but they were appalled by his tremendous appetite.

"I wish we could turn him out in the yard to forage for himself," Joanne sighed several days later as she peeled her second heaping pan of potatoes. "It's all I can do to keep one helping ahead of him!"

At first Mr. Abbott insisted upon remaining in the kitchen, teasing the girls as they worked and sampling the food. Then he fell into the habit of sitting on the front porch with Mrs. Salisbury and chatting with her for hours. Frequently they became involved in violent arguments about trivial matters just for diversion.

After one of their disagreements Mrs. Salisbury would maintain a stony silence which was refreshing. But Mr. Abbott would once again take refuge in the kitchen!

In spite of such slight annoyances, the days at Red Gate Farm passed very pleasantly. Nancy would go into town on various errands for the boarders and sometimes Mrs. Byrd.

One day she had just returned to the farm from a shopping trip and on her way to the house stopped at the mailbox.

"There might be a letter from Dad," she thought, and drew out a stack of mail.

She took it all into the house, where Mrs. Byrd asked Nancy to distribute the letters. As she was sorting them out, she came to one addressed to the Black Snake Colony.

"Look!" Nancy exclaimed. "This letter belongs to the nature cult. The mailman must have put it in our box by mistake."

"What will you do?" asked Bess seriously. "Drive over with it?"

"Of course not," growled Mr. Abbott, who had just entered the room. "You keep away from those outrageous people. Take it back to the post office."

Nancy studied the postmark. It was very blurred. Could it be Riverside Heights, or was she mistaken? Her curiosity about the mysterious cult was now even more aroused. Perhaps she could deliver the letter in person! But she got no further in her plan, for just then a neighbor passed on his way to town. Mrs. Byrd handed him the letter to remail.

Nancy felt disappointed, but was determined to find out in some way what was going on "over the hill." "If I can only be alone with Bess and George a little later, maybe we can come up with some plan" she thought.

There had been a letter from Mr. Drew, informing Nancy that he had returned home. "At least Dad's making progress on *his* case!" she said to herself.

Then Nancy hurried off to the barn where the "city slickers," as Reuben called them, were to have a milking lesson.

"It's no trick at all!" Bess insisted. "Give me that pail and I'll show you just how it's done."

Reuben handed over the bucket, and Bess marched determinedly up to the cow.

"Nice bossy," she murmured, giving the animal a timid pat on the neck.

The cow responded with a suspicious look and flirt of her tail. As Bess set down the milking stool, the cow kicked it over.

Bess sprang back in alarm. "You can't expect me to milk a vicious cow!" she exclaimed.

Joanne and Reuben exploded with laughter.

"Primrose is an extremely smart cow," Reuben drawled. "She won't stand being milked except from the side she's used to!"

Reluctantly Bess picked up the overturned stool and went around to the left side. The cow leisurely moved herself sideways.

"I give up! Here, you try it, George."

"Oh, no, Bess. I wouldn't spoil your fun for anything!"

After a great deal of maneuvering, Bess succeeded in handling the whole procedure to the satisfaction of Primrose. Nancy came last, and she, too, was a bit awkward. When Reuben finally sat down to do the milking, the girls watched him with admiration. "It just takes practice," he said, smiling.

That evening Mrs. Salisbury and Mr. Abbott

had their usual disagreement and both retired early. Mrs. Byrd soon followed, leaving the girls alone on the porch.

"Do you think there will be any activity on the hill tonight?" George asked suddenly.

"I'm not sure," Joanne answered. "But it's a good clear night and the moon is full, so the setting is perfect for it."

"I'm dying to see what those nature enthusiasts look like," added Bess. "Just so they don't come too close!"

It was a lovely evening and Nancy had been only half listening to the chatter. She remained silent and thoughtful. The letter addressed to the Black Snake Colony was still very much on her mind.

"What's up, Nancy?" Bess finally asked, noticing her friend's silence.

"Three guesses," Nancy replied with a laugh. "I'm still curious about that envelope I had in my hands this afternoon. I'm almost certain that blurred postmark read Riverside Heights."

"Even if it did," George remarked, "it could have been written by almost anyone and simply *mailed* in Riverside Heights."

"I suppose you're right," Nancy agreed. "I guess I'm trying too hard. But let's walk over toward the hill."

The four girls started off. They crossed one field in front of the house and were just climbing a rail fence to the next one when Nancy cried out:

"Am I seeing things? Look! Over there on that hill!"

Following her gaze, the girls were astonished to see shadowy white figures flitting about in the moonlight.

"Ghosts!" Bess exclaimed.

"Ghosts nothing," George retorted. "There's no such animal!"

"Don't be alarmed," Joanne said with a smile. "I imagine the members of the nature cult are having one of their festive airings by the light of the moon!"

The girls watched the cult members go through their mystic rites.

"They're not doing much of anything," Nancy observed, "except flapping around."

Within ten minutes the ceremony apparently was concluded. The white figures clustered together for a moment, then moved off across the hillside.

"I wonder where they're heading," Nancy mused. "Back to their tents?"

Joanne had been watching intently. Now she shook her head. "I don't think so. I forgot to tell you—the cave has another opening on the slope of the hill, near the river. The colony members are going in that direction."

Immediately Nancy's curiosity was aroused.

Did this mean the white-robed group intended to go into the cave itself? If so, why? To continue the ceremony?

"It certainly was a short performance," Bess remarked as the mysterious "dancers" vanished from sight. "I wonder if the ritual has any significance."

"That's what I'd like to know," Nancy said quietly. "And that's what we must find out!"

"Not tonight!" Joanne said firmly. "Grandmother will be very upset if we don't come right back."

Reluctantly Nancy gave up the idea. The girls started for the farmhouse, but Nancy kept looking back over her shoulder, determined not to miss anything. However, the hillside remained uninhabited and still.

As the girls drew near the road, the motor of a car broke the silence and headlights appeared. The automobile slowed down in front of the farmhouse as if about to stop. Then suddenly the car went on. Why? Nancy wondered. Had the driver seen the girls and changed his mind?

CHAPTER IX

Black Snake Colony Member

NANCY was too far away from the car to see its driver or license plate. Thoughtfully she went to bed, but lay awake for some time, feeling completely baffled over the many mysterious happenings.

By morning she felt eager for action. Ever since her arrival at Red Gate Farm, Nancy had wanted to visit the cavern on the hillside. The strange moonlight ceremony and the unidentified car which had hesitated in front of the house only intensified her interest in the place.

She broached the subject of a visit there to Mrs. Byrd, but Joanne's grandmother frowned on the idea. "I'll worry if you go," she said. "Those folks are probably harmless, but we don't know much about them. I wish now I had never rented the land. The neighbors are saying I was foolish to do it in the first place."

"And so you were!" Mrs. Salisbury, who had overheard the conversation, chimed in. "You'll ruin the value of your farm. Why, people around are saying dreadful things about the members of that cult. Even Reuben is afraid to go near the place!"

"I'm not," Nancy announced. "I think it would be fun to investigate."

Mrs. Salisbury snorted. "Fun! Girls these days have strange ideas of fun! First thing you know, Mrs. Byrd, she'll be wanting to join the colony!"

"Nonsense." Mrs. Byrd smiled.

In order to avoid further dissension, Nancy dropped the subject of the cave. But that afternoon she set out alone on a hike. Making her way to the woods which skirted the river, Nancy struck a well-worn path and decided to continue along it.

She had walked only a short way when the sound of a faint cry came to her. Nancy halted in the path and listened intently. The cry was not repeated.

"Maybe I imagined it," she said to herself.

Nevertheless, Nancy quickened her pace, looking about her as she walked. As she rounded a bend a few minutes later, she was startled to see a woman hunched over on the ground, writhing in pain.

"What's the matter?" Nancy cried out, hurrying over to her. Then the girl's eyes widened.

This was the woman she had seen running across a field the night of the storm.

"I tripped on a root in the path," the woman murmured, rocking back and forth in pain. "My ankle—it's broken."

Nancy dropped to one knee and quickly examined the injured ankle. It was swelling rapidly, but all the bones seemed to be in place.

"See if you can stand," she advised.

With Nancy's help the woman managed to get to her feet, but winced as she tried to take her first step.

"It isn't broken," Nancy said gently, "but you have a bad sprain."

"Oh, what'll I do now?" the woman moaned.

"Do you live far from here?" Nancy asked.

The stranger looked at her rather queerly and did not answer at once. Nancy thought she had not understood, so repeated the question.

"About a quarter of a mile up the river," was the mumbled response. "I'll get there all right."

"You're scarcely able to walk a step," Nancy said with a troubled frown. "Please let me run back to the farm and bring help."

"No, no," the woman protested, clutching Nancy fearfully by the arm. "I don't want to be a bother to anyone!"

"Nonsense! You shouldn't be walking at all. It won't take me a minute to get someone to help you."

The woman shook her head stubbornly. "My foot feels better now. I can walk by myself."

She started off, but nearly collapsed by the time she had taken three steps.

"If you won't let me go for help, then at least let me take you home."

Again the woman protested, but Nancy took hold of her arm and placed it over her own shoulder. With Nancy's support, the woman made slow and painful progress up the path.

"This is killing you," Nancy said, dismayed that the woman was so foolishly stubborn. "I can get our hired man to carry you—"

"No!" the woman objected vehemently.

Her unwillingness to accept help puzzled Nancy. As they made their way slowly along, she became aware that her companion's distress was not entirely due to pain, but partially to Nancy's own presence. This mystified Nancy, but she could not turn back as long as she knew the woman really needed her.

"I don't remember seeing any houses along the river," Nancy said after a time. "You're not a member of the nature cult, are you?"

A half-cynical expression crossed the woman's face, then one of sadness. "Yes," she returned quietly, "I'm one of the members."

Nancy took time to scrutinize her companion more carefully than before. She wore a blue gingham dress which was plain and durable, and certainly did not appear to be a costume. The woman did not speak or act as Nancy imagined a member of the cult would. She seemed like any other person.

"It must be healthful to live an outdoor life," Nancy remarked, feeling that some comment was necessary. "I've often looked over at your tents and thought I should like to visit the colony some time."

The woman stopped abruptly in the path and faced Nancy, an odd look on her face.

"You must never come near!"

"Why not?"

"It wouldn't be safe!"

"Not safe!" Nancy echoed in astonishment. "I don't understand."

"I—I mean the members of the cult don't want folks prying around," the woman said hastily.

"I see. The rites are secret?"

"That's it," the woman said in obvious relief.

"But why couldn't I visit the colony sometime when ceremonies aren't being held?" Nancy persisted.

"You mustn't come near the hillside—ever!" the stranger warned.

The two continued up the path. To Nancy it was apparent that her questions had disturbed the woman, for several times she caught her looking distressed and worried.

As they approached the hillside colony, and before they were within sight of the tents, the woman stopped short.

"Thank you for your help," she said quietly. "I can make it alone from here."

Nancy hesitated. The woman's firm tone told her it would do no good to protest. She was not going to let Nancy come any nearer the camp!

"At least let me find something that you can use as a cane," Nancy said.

She searched along the path and found a branch that was strong enough. The woman accepted it gratefully. Her face softened and she stood for an instant, looking intently at Nancy.

"You're a good girl to help a stranger like me. I wish—" The woman turned away abruptly. "Remember," she advised sternly over her shoulder, "don't ever come near the camp!"

Still perplexed, Nancy watched the woman hobble away. It took her a long time to reach the top of the hill, but at last she disappeared from sight.

"I can't understand why the poor thing acted the way she did," Nancy said to herself as she sat down on a log to think. "What harm could it have done if I'd gone with her to the colony? The cult must have some very important secrets!"

The more Nancy considered the matter, the more baffled she became.

"You must never come near the hillside!"
the stranger warned

"The woman didn't look as though being a member of the Black Snake Colony made her very happy," Nancy thought. "If they're so afraid that someone will discover their secrets, they must be doing more than just flitting at night in white robes! Maybe that's only to keep people from guessing what really goes on there!"

As Nancy reached this startling conclusion, she jumped up and walked briskly toward Red Gate Farm.

"There's one thing certain," she said to herself with a chuckle. "Now that the woman has forbidden me to go near the camp, I can't resist finding out what's happening there!"

Nancy was just approaching the farmhouse when she heard the phone ringing. She hurried inside and answered it.

"Yes, this is Nancy Drew," she replied to a strange man's question.

"One moment."

While Nancy waited, she wondered who the caller might be. Was someone going to threaten her to desist in her detective work?

"Oh!" she said as the next speaker announced himself as Chief McGinnis. A sense of relief came over the girl.

"I have some news, Nancy," the officer said. "It's discouraging. Nothing on the code or the missing men." Then he chuckled. "We need another clue from you."

Nancy realized her old friend was teasing. "Glad to help," she said gaily. "What's the assignment?"

"To find out where the Hale Syndicate moved to after it left Room 305."

"Then that was their headquarters!" Nancy cried excitedly.

"Temporarily. But they left no forwarding address," the police chief said.

"If we could decipher the rest of the code we might be able to trace them," Nancy said. "Anyhow, I'll be on the lookout for any clues. At least it shouldn't be too hard to find Yvonne Wong."

Chief McGinnis agreed and assured Nancy he would let her know if there were any new developments. Then he asked, "And what are you doing? Any mysteries up your way?"

"There might be." She told him the little she had been able to glean about the mysterious nature cult. She described the unusual moonlight ceremony the girls had witnessed and the appearance of the unidentified car.

The police chief whistled in amazement. "Sounds as though you *do* have another mystery up your sleeve! Have you come across any possible clues to what the cult is worshiping, Nancy?"

The girl detective hesitated a moment before telling Chief McGinnis about her curious conversation with the woman she had assisted in the woods. She decided to mention it, and added that although the woman had readily admitted to being a member of the cult, she had given Nancy no reason for her firm warning to stay away from the meeting place.

"Black Snake Colony, eh?" the police chief said reflectively.

"Yes," Nancy replied. "Have you ever heard of it?"

"No, but let me look in a report we have here on all cults. I'll call you right back."

Nancy waited eagerly for the phone to ring. When it did she snatched up the receiver. "The Black Snake Colony is not listed," Chief Mc-Ginnis told her.

"You mean it's a phony?" Nancy asked excitedly.

CHAPTER X

Plan of Attack

CHIEF MCGINNIS refused to comment on the possibility that the Black Snake Colony might be a phony group.

"They may not have been in existence long enough to be known," he replied. "But you might try to find out what you can and let me know."

"I'll do that," the young detective agreed.

After Nancy had put down the phone, she reflected for a long minute on the new twist to the hillside mystery, then walked out to the front porch, where Mrs. Salisbury, Mr. Abbott, and the three girls were seated.

Nancy had not planned to tell them of her experience, but her face was so animated it revealed her thoughts. They besieged her with questions until finally she revealed her meeting with the woman member of the strange nature cult.

"Told you not to come near, did she?" Mrs. Salisbury cackled. "Well, I hope you intend to follow her advice."

Nancy laughed and shook her head. "I'm more interested than ever in what's going on up there on the hillside. I'm ready for a little adventure right about now!"

"So am I," George chimed in.

Joanne nodded vigorously, while Bess, always more cautious, agreed rather halfheartedly.

"Better stay away," Mr. Abbott advised, for once not contradicting Mrs. Salisbury. "You can't tell what may be going on there."

Nancy was tempted to comment, but instead she forced a smile and said, "It seems to me that this matter may be of deep concern to Jo and her grandmother, if not to me."

Mrs. Byrd had stepped to the porch door in time to get the gist of the conversation, and at once spoke up.

"I think Nancy is right," she declared thoughtfully. "Of course, I don't want the girls to go looking for trouble, but I'm beginning to think someone ought to investigate those mysterious people. If anything questionable is going on, I want to know about it. I'll ask the Black Snake Colony to move out, even if I do lose the rent. Why, I might get into trouble myself if they stay."

Mr. Abbott and Mrs. Salisbury fell into ⌐injured silence. Nancy gave her friends a sly wink, and in a few minutes they all quietly withdrew to the springhouse to discuss their plans. Here, she told the girls about her conversation with Chief McGinnis.

"Something peculiar is going on at those cult meetings, I'm sure," Nancy went on, "and I must find out about them if I can. Do you all want to join me in the investigation?"

"Of course," Joanne and George said.

"Do you think it'll be safe?" Bess asked.

"I'm not making any rash promises." Nancy laughed.

Bess gave a little shiver. "I don't like it, but count me in."

"How can we visit the colony without being caught?" George asked.

"That's the problem," Nancy replied. "We must make our plans carefully. Before we do anything, I suggest we find out about the robes the cult members wear. We may need to wear similar ones to help us in our investigation."

"There's only one way to find that out," Joanne said. "Some night when they're having a ceremonial meeting, we can sneak through the woods and try to get a closer look at what's going on."

Nancy nodded excitedly. "The double entrance to the cave will be perfect!" she said. "If we can't sneak into the meetings any other way, we can get into the cave at the end they don't use."

"Sounds terribly risky to me!" Bess commented.

"Oh, for Pete's sake," George said scornfully. "Don't be such a wet blanket, Bess!"

Her cousin opened her mouth to retort, but Nancy interposed quickly to forestall any further argument.

"We'd better not tell our plan to anyone except your grandmother, Jo," she advised. "Otherwise, Mrs. Salisbury and Mr. Abbott will try to talk her out of letting us investigate."

After a light supper and some rather forced conversation on trivial matters, the girls retired. They had tried to keep silent about the activities of the nature cult, but their secretive manner did not escape the notice of Mrs. Salisbury and Mr. Abbott.

"You're up to something," Mrs. Salisbury remarked the next morning. "And if I were Mrs. Byrd, I'd put a stop to it at once!"

Mrs. Byrd, however, went on serenely with her work, being careful not to interfere with the girls' plans. They maintained a close watch of the hillside, but for two days seldom saw anyone in the vicinity.

"I think they've holed in for the rest of the

summer," George declared impatiently at breakfast. "Either that, or they've moved out."

"The cult's still there," Joanne reassured her.
"The rent check arrived in the morning mail."

"By the way, where do these nature people get
their food?" Nancy queried. "They can't live on
blue sky and inspiration."

"I think friends must bring food to them in
automobiles," Joanne answered. "Several times
I've seen swanky cars drive up and park near the
hillside."

"The cult members must be fairly well off,
then," Nancy said thoughtfully. "I'm getting
tired of marking time. I wish something would
happen soon. If it doesn't, I think I'll investigate
that cave, anyway!"

That night the girls were late in finishing the
dishes. By the time they had put everything
away it was quite dark. When they went out to
the porch, they were relieved to find that the
boarders had gone to their rooms.

The girls sat talking quietly for some time.
The moon was high, and Nancy, from force of
habit, glanced eagerly toward the distant hill.

"Look, girls!" she exclaimed. "They're at it
again!"

The four girls could see white objects moving
to and fro, apparently going through a weird
ritual. Nancy sprang to her feet.

"We'll have to hurry if we want to see anything," she said. "Come on! We'll take the short cut!"

They dashed across the lawn, flung open the gate, and ran through the woods. Nancy led the way up the river path, then to the sparsely wooded hillside. Not until they were close to the camp did she stop.

"We'll have to be very careful," she warned in a whisper. "Scatter and hide behind trees. And don't make a sound."

The girls obeyed, Bess staying as close to George as possible. Nancy found a huge oak tree well up the hill, and hid behind it. From this vantage point she could see fairly well.

Nancy had been there for less than five minutes when she heard the sound of several cars approaching. They came up the woods road and stopped at the foot of the hill, not far from the nature camp.

Several men stepped from the cars. Nancy was too far away to see their faces, but she did observe that they quickly donned long white robes with head masks, and joined the other costumed figures who were on the brow of the hill.

For nearly ten minutes the members of the cult flitted back and forth, waving their arms and making weird noises. Then they moved single file toward the cavern and vanished.

Suddenly Nancy felt herself grasped by an arm. She wheeled sharply and then laughed softly.

"George! For goodness sake, don't ever do that again! You scared me silly!"

"What do you make of it, Nancy?"

"It's the strangest thing I've ever seen. I haven't been able to figure it out."

"What should we do next?" asked Bess, who had joined them.

"Let's follow them into the cave!" George proposed rashly.

"And be caught?" Nancy returned. "No, this is serious business. I think it's time to go home and plan our own costumes."

"I wonder why so many people came here in automobiles?" Joanne mused, as the girls walked off slowly.

"That's what I've been wondering," Nancy replied soberly, "but I think I might know."

"Why?" her friends demanded.

"It looks to me as if only a few persons are actually living in the Black Snake Colony. Apparently they want to give the impression that the organization is a large one, so they have these other people come the night set for the ceremonials."

"There were certainly a lot of men in those cars," added Bess.

"Why should they go to all that trouble?" Joanne asked doubtfully.

"I don't know," Nancy admitted, "unless it's because they're trying to hide something they're doing here." She changed the subject. "I think we'll be able to make costumes like theirs if you'll give us some old pillowcases and sheets, Jo. When we visit the cave, we must disguise ourselves to make our scheme work!"

CHAPTER XI

A Midnight Message

"When shall we visit the cave?" George asked.

"As soon as we can," Nancy answered. "Of course we must help Jo and her grandmother with the work."

Since there was no further evidence of activity on the hillside, the girls went to bed.

The next morning George remarked, as she helped Nancy make her bed, "What do you suppose those men do between ceremonials? It certainly is strange how much time they spend in that cave!"

"What puzzles me is those automobiles that were on the hillside," Bess said. "Why did they come? Surely those men were here for something besides ballet dancing. What's your guess, Nancy?"

"I'm afraid I haven't any answer. But I mean to find one for Mrs. Byrd's and Jo's sakes."

The three girls learned that Reuben was due to be absent most of the day and offered to do his chores. During the morning they picked cherries and took them to town to sell at a local market. When they returned, a small, strange car was standing in the driveway. Loud voices were coming from the living room.

"I don't have to sell and I won't sell!" Mrs. Byrd said with finality in her tone.

"That's what you think," a man said sneeringly. "You're going to lose this farm and I can buy it cheaper from the bank. Why don't you sell it to me and make a little profit? Then you can go to the city and take life easy."

"We don't want to go to the city," Joanne spoke up. "We're getting along all right here. More boarders are coming soon and we are paying off our back mortgage interest. So we don't have to sell."

Outside, Nancy, Bess, and George looked at one another. The insistent buyer again! Fervently they hoped that Mrs. Byrd would not weaken in her decision. A moment later they felt relieved.

"I will say good afternoon, Mr. Kent," Mrs. Byrd said. "Thank you for your offer, but I cannot accept it."

"You'll be sorry! You'll regret this!" the caller stormed. He came out the screen door, slamming it viciously behind him.

Nancy stared in surprise. Mr. Kent certainly was one of the most ill-mannered men she had ever seen! And also, she thought wryly, one of the most tenacious! Why was he so determined to buy the Byrd home?

Mr. Kent, his face red with anger, stepped into his car and sped off, but not before he gave Nancy and her friends a baleful look. "Nice disposition," George commented sarcastically.

"I hope he never shows up again," Bess said firmly.

The girls found Mrs. Byrd and Joanne quite shaken. "I can't understand that man's persistence," the woman said.

Nancy was sure the matter was tied in with the cult on the hillside but did not mention this theory. She merely said, "Try not to worry about Mr. Kent. I doubt that he'll return."

Soon the incident was forgotten as preparations for supper were started and the farm animals were fed. George elected to take care of gathering eggs from the henhouse. Bess gave the horse hay and water.

"I'll get the cow," Nancy offered, and went off toward the pasture to drive Primrose in.

But the cow was not there. Nancy walked around the fence surrounding the field to see if there was any opening through which the animal might have wandered. Finally she found one, and saw hoofprints leading toward a patch of woods.

Nancy dashed off among the trees. She had never been that way before, but there was only one path to follow. Several times she paused to listen and thought she heard the faint tinkling of a cowbell somewhere ahead of her.

It was rapidly growing dusky in the woods and Nancy hurried on. Again she stopped to listen. She could hear the cowbell distinctly now.

"Primrose can't be far ahead," she thought in relief, and went in that direction. Nancy finally caught sight of the Jersey contentedly munching grass on the hillside beyond.

Nancy stopped short and gave a gasp of astonishment—the sound of the cowbell had brought her to the mouth of the cave!

"I can hardly believe it!" she almost exclaimed aloud. This must be the other opening near the nature camp Jo told me about!"

Eagerly Nancy rushed toward the cave. But no sooner had she peered into the dark entrance than she was startled by the crackling of a twig behind her. Nancy wheeled to find a man standing not three feet away from her!

He seemed to have risen from the bushes which half hid the opening of the cave. Instantly it flashed through Nancy's mind that he had been stationed there to see that intruders did not enter.

"What're you doing here?" he asked, his voice as cold as steel.

Nancy recoiled. The man stood in the shadows of the shrubbery so that she could not see his face distinctly. But at the sound of his voice she knew instantly she was in danger.

"I must persuade him I wasn't spying," she thought desperately.

"Better speak up!" the man snarled. "What're you doin' here, girlie?"

"I was hunting for that cow," Nancy replied as casually as possible. She pointed to the Jersey, which was grazing a short distance away.

She held her ground defiantly. There was a moment's silence. Nancy could feel that the man was staring at her, as if undecided whether or not to believe her.

"So you were after the cow?" the lookout growled. "Then why are you by this cave?"

"Why, I was just wondering what was inside," Nancy said innocently. "Surely there's no harm in looking."

"You've no business around here!" the man snapped. "This property belongs to the members of the Black Snake Colony."

"Oh!" Nancy exclaimed in pretended awe. "Then you must belong to the colony. How very interesting!"

The man made no response to Nancy's remark. Instead, he muttered:

"Round up that old cow of yours and get out of here! And don't come trespassing again!"

Nancy knew she would gain nothing by arguing. Obediently she overtook the cow and headed her back toward Red Gate. The man watched until Nancy disappeared into the woods.

As soon as she had started the cow down the path, however, Nancy quietly retraced her steps. She reached the edge of the woods just in time to catch a glimpse of the man entering the cave.

"That proves he's one of the Black Snake group," she told herself. "He was acting as a guard for them."

For an instant Nancy was tempted to follow, but common sense told her not to press her luck. The lookout seemed determined enough to make trouble for her if she took the chance. Reluctantly, the young sleuth turned back toward the farm.

It was clear to Nancy that the entire business of the Black Snake group was anything but open and aboveboard! Obviously they were afraid that some of the countryfolk would attempt to investigate.

When Nancy finally reached the barn and Joanne began to milk Primrose, the other girls plied their friend with questions.

"We were beginning to worry," Joanne said in relief. "I wouldn't have let you go alone if I'd known this cow of ours would stray so far."

"I'm glad I went," Nancy said quickly.

She then told the others what had taken place

near the mouth of the cave. They gasped in astonishment upon hearing of her encounter with the lookout.

"Weren't you frightened when he sprang up out of nowhere?" Bess asked, giving Nancy an admiring glance. "I'd have fainted on the spot!"

"That's an easy way out if I ever heard one!" Nancy commented with a laugh.

"Girls don't faint these days," George scoffed. "Probably you'd have screamed and brought all the members down on you. They'd have dragged you off and put an end to you!"

"Thanks, George," Bess muttered. "You say the nicest things!"

"Well, girls, talk all you like," Nancy added, "but don't lose your nerve altogether. I still want to get a closer look at that cave!"

"Not tonight!" Bess said firmly.

Nancy smiled. "I hope there won't be a ritual on the hillside tonight. We've been too busy to get our costumes ready."

The girls watched but the distant landscape remained dark. Finally they went to bed. Not long afterward, Nancy was roused from a fitful slumber by the stopping of a car not far from her window. She hopped from bed and went to peer out. A tall, slender woman who wore her hair piled high was walking to the front door.

Nancy leaned out the window and called, "What is it you wish?"

"Nancy Drew. Is she here?"

"Yes, I'm Nancy."

"I have a letter for you." Nancy did not recognize the woman's voice. But she might be disguising it.

"From whom?"

"Your father."

"Why are you bringing it now?"

"It's an urgent message," the strange woman said. "I'll leave it on the doorstep."

She dropped the letter, hurried into the car, and the man at the wheel drove off. Heart pounding, Nancy put on her robe and slippers and hurried down to the front door.

CHAPTER XII

Secret Service Agents

THE stopping of the car at the house had awakened Mrs. Byrd who slept on the first floor. She met Nancy in the hall and asked what was happening.

Quickly Nancy told her, then opened the door. On the porch lay a plain envelope with Nancy's name typed on it.

"This seems like a peculiar way for your father to get in touch with you," Mrs. Byrd remarked. "Why didn't he phone if it's urgent?"

"I don't understand it myself," Nancy answered, as she tore open the letter.

The message was typewritten and was succinct. Nancy was to return home at once. Her father needed her. She was not to try to communicate with him. He could not explain why. It was signed "Dad."

Nancy read the letter to Mrs. Byrd. "Oh, I

couldn't let you start out at this time of night alone," the woman said at once. "You must wait until morning."

"This whole thing doesn't seem like Dad," Nancy reflected. "He wouldn't send a terse note like this even if he *were* in some kind of trouble."

Mrs. Byrd was very much concerned. "It seems to me he would have called you on the phone in an emergency," she offered thoughtfully.

"Yes," Nancy agreed, "that's why this puzzles me so. But don't you worry about it, Mrs. Byrd. This is something I'll have to try to figure out myself."

"But, my dear," Mrs. Byrd repeated, "it's impossible for you to do anything about it at this hour."

Nancy carefully studied the note again. Suddenly she became aware of a familiar scent of perfume. The young detective held the envelope to her nostrils. It had been handled by someone who used the distinctive Blue Jade scent which Bess had purchased!

Instantly Nancy was alerted. "It wouldn't surprise me, Mrs. Byrd, if this letter is a phony! I'm going to call Dad, even though it's an unearthly hour to waken him."

She picked up the receiver in the hall. No sound reached her ears. "I'm afraid the line is dead," she told Mrs. Byrd. "Does this happen often?"

"It has never happened before," Mrs. Byrd said. "I made a call after supper and everything was all right then."

Nancy stood in perplexed silence. Had her father tried to get her, found the line out of order, then given the note to the couple? The woman might have carried the letter in a handbag which contained a purse-size bottle of the Oriental perfume.

"In that case I ought to start for River Heights," Nancy thought. But a feeling of suspicion about the whole thing overpowered her. It might be a trap. The telephone line could have been cut. One or more persons might try to capture her on the road.

"But why?" Nancy asked herself repeatedly. She came to the conclusion that the Hale Syndicate was back of the incident. They must have found out she had reported her suspicions to the police and somehow had learned where she was staying.

She turned to Mrs. Byrd and said, "I'll wait until seven o'clock, then try the phone again. If it still isn't working, I'll go to town and call Dad."

"Thank you, dear." Mrs. Byrd patted Nancy on the shoulder. "But don't go anywhere alone. Take Bess and George with you."

"I will."

Promptly at seven o'clock Nancy tried to get in touch with her father but the phone still was not working. Joanne was already up, but Nancy roused Bess and George. The three girls were astounded to learn about the note.

"We'll get breakfast in town," Nancy told Mrs. Byrd as she prepared to drive off with her friends. "And if I don't have to go to River Heights, I can do your shopping, too. Suppose you give me the list."

Halfway to town, George said suddenly, "Nancy, isn't your gasoline tank nearly empty?"

Nancy nodded. "I'm glad you reminded me. Watch for a station and we'll stop."

Presently Bess sighted one on the main road. "It's the same place we stopped to eat on our way to the farm," she said.

"So it is," George remarked.

"I can phone from here," Nancy decided.

She turned in at the gravel driveway, but as two other cars were ahead of her, she drew up some distance from the pump.

"How about getting breakfast here after you phone?" Bess suggested.

The girls agreed. Bess and George entered the lunchroom while Nancy went to an outdoor phone booth. She had her father on the wire in a few moments.

"Dad, did you send me a note last night?"

"Why, no."

Quickly his daughter explained her question.

The lawyer said grimly, "It's plain to see someone wants to harm you in one way or another. Please be very careful."

Nancy promised and said, "Anyway, I'm glad you're all right."

After Nancy hung up, she dialed the phone company to report that the Byrd line was out of order. A few minutes later she joined Bess and George at a table and whispered the result of her conversation with Mr. Drew.

"Oh, Nancy, this means you're in danger!" Bess said worriedly.

"I thought at least I'd be safe at Red Gate Farm," Nancy said.

"I wonder," George muttered.

The girls were the only customers in the restaurant. No one came to wait on them. From an inner room, evidently used as an office, they could hear excited voices.

"Something's wrong," Nancy said to her companions.

Just then two men came out of the office in company with the gasoline-station attendant and the woman who served as waitress of the restaurant. The woman was talking excitedly.

"We found the twenty-dollar bill in the cash register at the end of the day. It looked like any other money, and we didn't suspect anything was wrong until John took the day's receipts to the bank. And of all things they said the bill was counterfeit and they'd have to turn it over to the Secret Service!"

"Yes," one of the agents spoke up, "we've just come from the bank and it's a counterfeit all right. There's been a lot of this bad money passed lately. The forgery is very clever."

"What am I going to do?" the woman cried. "We were cheated out of twenty dollars! It isn't fair to hard-working people like John and me. Aren't you Secret Service agents going to do something about it?"

"We're doing all we can," one of the men replied. "We don't have much to go on."

"It was a girl who gave me the bill," the woman explained. "There were several of them in the party. I'd recognize— Oh!" she shrieked. "There's the very girl!" She pointed an accusing finger at Nancy Drew.

Nancy and her friends stared in astonishment. They could not believe what they had just heard.

"Arrest that girl!" the woman screamed. "Don't let any of them get away—they're all in on it together!"

"Just a minute," one of the agents said. "Suppose you explain," he suggested to Nancy.

The excited woman, however, was not to be calmed. She rushed toward Nancy and shook her fist at the girl. "Don't deny you gave me that phony bill!" she almost screamed.

"I neither deny nor affirm it," Nancy said, turning to the agents. "I did give the woman a twenty-dollar bill, but how do you know it was the counterfeit?"

"It was the only twenty we took in that day," the waitress retorted.

Nancy's thoughts raced. "I'll take your word for it," she said quietly.

Opening her purse she took out another twenty-dollar bill. The woman snatched the money and handed it to one of the Secret Service men. "Is this good?" she asked crisply.

The agent examined the bill. Then he looked at Nancy. "Where did you get this?"

"From my father. He gave me both bills, as a matter of fact. One was for car emergencies."

Instead of giving the bill to the woman, the man put it into his pocket. "This is serious business, young lady. The bill you just gave me is also counterfeit!"

Nancy was thunderstruck. Bess and George gasped. Before any of them could speak, the lunchroom woman cried out, "She's one of the gang! Arrest her!"

For the first time the station attendant spoke up. "Take it easy, Liz. These girls don't exactly look like counterfeiters."

Liz sniffed. "People don't usually go around paying for sundaes with twenty-dollar bills!" she said tartly.

"My father gave me the money because I was going on a vacation."

"A likely story!" the woman sneered.

"It's the truth!" George spoke up indignantly. "The idea of accusing my friend of passing bad money on purpose! It's ridiculous!"

"Ridiculous, is it?" the woman retorted angrily. "You'll sing a different tune when you're in jail!"

"You can't have Nancy arrested. She didn't realize it was counterfeit money!" Bess protested. "George and I have some cash. We'll pay you twenty good dollars to make up for the bad one."

As the cousins pooled their funds and handed over the money, the woman quieted down. "Maybe I was a little hasty," she admitted. But she was not entirely cowed. "How about your fa-

ther?" she asked Nancy. "How come *he* had counterfeit bills?"

Nancy said she did not know, but certainly he had not acquired them dishonestly.

One of the Secret Service men said, "Suppose you tell us who you are, and—"

"I'll tell you who she is!" came an authoritative voice from the doorway.

CHAPTER XIII

A Hesitant Hitchhiker

UNOBSERVED by the girls, an automobile had driven up and parked near the filling station. A tall young man had alighted and started for the lunchroom. Upon hearing the amazing conversation inside, he had halted. Then, realizing Nancy was in need of help, he had stepped inside.

"Karl!" Nancy cried out. She had never before been so glad to see anyone!

"It looks as if I just got here in the nick of time." Karl Abbott Jr. smiled.

"They're trying to arrest us!" Bess exclaimed.

"You're kidding!" Karl cried in astonishment.

"It's no joke," Nancy returned earnestly, then told him of her predicament.

"Look here," Karl said bluntly, turning to the two Secret Service agents, "you can't hold these girls."

"Who are you?" one of the agents demanded.

"My name is Karl Abbott, and these girls are friends of mine. As it happens, my father is living at Red Gate Farm in Round Valley, where they also are staying. I was on my way there when I thought I'd stop for a bite to eat. Lucky I did, too!"

"These girls may be friends of yours," the unpleasant woman spoke up shrilly, "but this girl had better explain why she gave me counterfeit money!"

"If you're accusing these girls of deliberately trying to pass counterfeit money, you're crazy!" Karl Abbott cried out.

"You're willing to vouch for the honesty of this young lady's father as well?" the agent asked.

"Most definitely. This is Nancy Drew. No doubt you've heard of her father, the famous lawyer. If you haven't, you soon will!"

"Not Carson Drew of River Heights?"

"Yes," Karl replied.

"Why didn't you tell us who you were?" the restaurant owner asked.

"You didn't give me a chance to tell you anything!" Nancy retorted. "And you didn't seem ready to believe what I did have to say."

The two agents looked at each other. One asked to see Nancy's driver's license, then with a smile he said, "Too bad you have such a loss because of the counterfeit money. The outfit which is distributing the twenty-dollar bills is a clever one.

"The money is turning up in many places. I'll get in touch with your father to find out where he was given the bills. Incidentally, we understand a few women are mixed up in the racket. That's why we detained you."

"Let's get out of here!" George urged.

The girls hurriedly left the lunchroom with Karl. The government agents leisurely followed them outside.

As Nancy was about to step into her car, she thought of something. It occurred to her that by some remote chance the investigators might be interested in the phony message which she had brought with her.

"This may or may not have anything to do with the case," she told them, handing over the scented note. "But the signature is a forgery, and the perfume has some mystery to it."

She gave a brief account of her own involvement with the mystery, beginning with her encounter on the train with the man who had mentioned "the Chief," and ending with the code.

"If the rest of the code can be deciphered," Nancy concluded, "that might give us the answer to everything, including the Hale Syndicate's whereabouts."

"So you're the young detective Chief McGinnis mentioned in his reports to us," one of the agents said admiringly. "What you've done so far is really astounding. Chief McGinnis didn't mention you by name. He probably figured you would prefer him not to.

"Your deductions seem very sound, Miss Drew, and I'd advise you to be careful. That Hale gang may think you know too much already. I'll take this note and pass it along to a handwriting expert. Perhaps Yvonne Wong was the person who delivered it."

Nancy shook her head. "From what I could see of the woman, I know she wasn't Yvonne."

After the agent had wished Nancy luck on the solution of the mystery, she said good-by to the men, and, with the others, went back to her car.

Although Karl Abbott was eager to continue on to Red Gate Farm to see his father, he expressed concern about the three girls and their upsetting experience. He asked for a detailed account of the events which had led to Nancy's predicament. He was most interested and sympathetic when the girls told him the whole story.

"Well," he said admiringly, "I guess I won't worry too much about you girls. You certainly aren't easily daunted by emergencies."

After Karl Jr. and the trio had exchanged good-bys, the young man got into his car and drove on to the farm.

Bess turned to her companions. "Where to? I'm more starved than ever."

"It's only a short way to town from here," Nancy replied. "We can get breakfast there and then do our shopping."

Soon the girls reached Round Valley. When they finished eating, Nancy looked at Mrs. Byrd's list.

"There's really not much on it," she commented. "Two of us could do the shopping. Suppose you girls take over and I'll go buy the material for our costumes."

"Material?" Bess queried.

Nancy laughed. "If we're going to join the Black Snake group in one of their rites, we'll need ghost costumes, and I've decided it wouldn't be fair to Mrs. Byrd to ruin four of her sheets and pillowcases."

Suddenly George said, "What are we going to use for money?"

Nancy had only two dollars. Bess and George between them counted six.

"That will pay for the meat and groceries," Bess said. "I guess our costume material and the other errands will have to wait."

The food shopping was soon finished and the girls returned to Red Gate Farm.

Joanne met them at the kitchen door. "Guess what?" she burst out. "The telephone repairman was here. He said our line had been cut!"

Nancy nodded. "By those people who were here last night."

"I suppose so. Oh, Nancy, I'm so worried for you. And Karl Jr. tells us you've had another adventure this morning. He said you'd explain."

Nancy, with lively interruptions from Bess and George, related the girls' recent experience.

"I gave those Secret Service men the note and told them the Hale Syndicate might be mixed up in some way with the counterfeiters. The syndicate may be the distributors of the phony bills."

"Well, do let the authorities take care of it," Joanne urged. "I want you girls to have a good time while you're here."

"Oh, I'm having a wonderful time," Nancy assured her. "By the way, I think we should work on our costumes for the hillside ceremony. Could you repay us the money we spent today so I can buy more material? We decided it isn't fair to use your grandmother's good linens."

"Oh, yes, right away. I'll get it from Gram. And I think there are a few more groceries she needs."

Joanne returned in a few minutes and handed over the money to which she added enough for the marketing. Nancy headed for town. She had gone about a mile when she sighted a woman hurrying along the side of the country road. She was limping slightly.

"I'll offer her a ride," Nancy decided. "She seems to be in a great hurry."

She halted the car and called, "May I give you a lift to town?"

The woman glanced up, startled. Nancy was surprised to see that she was the woman from the Black Snake Colony whom she had helped several days before on the river trail! What she was doing so far from her camp Nancy did not know, but she was determined to make the most of the opportunity at hand.

"Please get in," Nancy urged, as the woman hesitated. "I'm sure your foot must be paining you. I notice that you are still limping."

"Thanks," the woman returned gratefully, hobbling over to the car door which Nancy held open for her. "I am in a hurry to get to town."

Before stepping inside she looked quickly over her shoulder as though fearing that someone might observe her actions.

She sighed in relief and settled back, looking very pale and exhausted.

"You weren't intending to walk all the way to town?" Nancy asked in a friendly, conversational tone.

The woman nodded. "I had to get there somehow."

"But aren't the members of your colony permitted to use any of the cars I've seen around the camp?" Nancy questioned, watching her companion closely and hoping that she might tactfully glean some information.

"We aren't allowed much freedom," the woman answered.

"You shouldn't be walking on that foot yet," Nancy protested. "You're apt to injure your ankle permanently."

"It's nearly well now," the woman told her, avoiding Nancy's eyes. "They didn't know at the camp that I was going to town. I—I left in a hurry."

Again the stranger cast an anxious glance over her shoulder. "She obviously thinks she's being followed," Nancy thought to herself. "Perhaps she's even running away!"

Nancy wanted to ask her companion a number of questions but the woman's aloofness discouraged her. Deciding on an entirely different course, the young sleuth pretended not to pay particular attention to the woman. For some time they drove along in silence. Nancy could see that her passenger was gradually relaxing and losing her fear.

"Am I going too fast for you?" Nancy inquired, thinking the time was right to launch the conversation.

"Oh, no," the woman returned quickly. "You can't go too fast for me." She hesitated, and then added, "I have an important letter to mail."

"Why don't you drop it in one of the roadside mailboxes?" Nancy suggested casually. "The rural carrier will pick it up and save you a long trip."

"I want to get it off this morning if I possibly can."

"I'll be glad to go to the post office and mail it for you," Nancy said, purposely drawing the woman out.

"Thank you, but no," the woman mumbled. "I— I'd feel better if I did it myself." As Nancy did not reply, she said, "I don't mean to be ungrateful for all you've done—really I don't. It's only that I mustn't get you into trouble."

"How could I get into trouble by helping you?" Nancy asked with a smile.

"You don't understand," her companion replied nervously. "There are things I can't explain. The leaders of the colony will be very angry with me if they find I have left even for a few hours, and especially that I've mailed this letter to my sister. The cult forbids communication with the outside world."

"I can't understand why you tolerate such rigid supervision," Nancy said impatiently. "Why, the leader of the cult must treat you as prisoners!"

"You're not far from wrong," the woman confessed.

"Then why don't you run away?"

The question startled the woman. She glanced sharply at Nancy, then as quickly looked away.

"I would if I dared," she said finally.

"Why don't you dare?" Nancy challenged. "I'll help you."

"No, you mustn't get mixed up in this. Perhaps later I can get away."

"I don't see what anyone can do to you if you decide to leave the colony," Nancy went on. "Surely you're a free person."

"Not any more," her companion returned sadly. "I'm in it too deep now. I'll have to go on until Fate helps me."

"I wouldn't wait," Nancy advised bluntly. "Let me help you—right now!"

CHAPTER XIV

Disturbing Gossip

THE strange woman in Nancy's car seemed to waver for a moment, as if about to accept the girl's offer of help. Then she shook her head.

"No, I won't drag you into it!" she said with finality. "You don't know what you'd be getting into if you helped me. Why, if they even learn that you've aided me in mailing this letter—"

Nancy saw the woman shudder. For one fleeting instant she, too, felt afraid—afraid of something she could not define.

The young sleuth realized that the woman was trying to warn her of danger. Nancy knew the wise thing to do was forget all about the nature cult and the strange things which apparently went on in the hillside cave. Yet, she felt that she was on the verge of discovering an important secret.

Nancy's companion was obviously relieved

when the car rounded a bend and brought them within sight of town. "If you'll just drop me off at the post office, I'll be most grateful," the woman said.

"May I take you back with me?" Nancy asked. "I'll be returning in less than an hour."

"No, I'll walk back."

Nancy saw that it was useless to protest and let the matter rest. She made no comment.

After leaving her passenger in front of the post office, Nancy continued down the main street to the supermarket. Later, while she waited in the check-out line to pay for her groceries, two women took their places behind her. They were talking earnestly together, and did not pay any attention to Nancy. She, in turn, did not notice them until one of the shoppers began to speak on a startling subject.

"It beats me the way those people carry on," she heard one of them say. "You'd think Mrs. Byrd would turn them out!"

Instantly Nancy became alert.

"I suppose she needs the money," the other woman responded, "but someone should speak to her about it. The idea of those folks capering around in bedclothes! They must be crazy!"

"That's just what I think!" the first woman remarked. "If I lived near that farm I wouldn't feel safe! And I don't think it's decent for a law-abiding community like ours to have folks like

that around. I'm going to get a big group together
and call on Mrs. Byrd to tell her what we think
of her!"

"I'll certainly join you," the woman said.

Nancy felt the situation was becoming serious;
that the criticism of Mrs. Byrd would grow even
sharper. If the two women carried out their
threat, the consequences might be very unpleasant. Prospective Red Gate boarders might change
their minds! The colony might take reprisals!

"One thing is certain," Nancy decided. "Our
costumes must be ready by tonight in case the
colony members have a meeting."

She paid for the groceries and went directly to
the material shop, where she bought several
yards of white muslin, then started for home.

Driving back to Red Gate Farm, Nancy kept a
sharp lookout for the woman from the Black
Snake Colony, but she was nowhere along the
road. "I wish I could have talked to her more. It
might have helped in my plan to attend the
ceremony."

Joanne, Bess, and George were just returning
from the woods with pails brimming over with
luscious-looking berries when Nancy drove into
the barnyard. As they started to help her carry
in the packages, Karl Abbott Jr. rushed gallantly
from the house to assist. He glanced curiously at
the soft, fat one which Nancy kept tucked under
her arm, but she did not give any explanation of

its contents. Besides, the elder Mr. Abbott and Mrs. Salisbury were within hearing distance.

Immediately after a late lunch and some pleasant conversation with the guests, Nancy excused herself and summoned the other girls to her room. There she unwrapped the material and brought out scissors, needles, and thread.

"We must work like mad," she said, "in case there's a meeting tonight."

With great excitement and anticipation she cut out the first costume which was to serve as an entering wedge to the nature-cult ceremonial. As Nancy worked, she told the story of her adventure with her passenger and the conversation of the women in the market.

Joanne was alarmed. "Oh, Gram must never hear of this!" she exclaimed. "She'd be heartbroken!"

The others agreed. "We won't tell Mrs. Byrd any more than we have to," George said. "I do hope we can solve the mystery before something ugly happens!"

For the next few hours their needles flew furiously. At last the costumes were finished. The four friends could not control their laughter as they tried them on.

"You certainly look as if you're ready for Halloween!" George told Nancy.

"Do you think I'll pass?"

"In the moonlight they won't be able to tell you from a full-fledged member of the cult," Bess declared. "Let's see you go through the mystic rites."

To the delight of her chums, Nancy danced around the room, waving her arms wildly and making weird moans.

"Jo!" a voice called. "Dinner's ready!"

Startled, the girls scrambled out of the white robes and hastily hid them. They tried to compose their faces as they hurried downstairs, but merely succeeded in looking guilty.

"Seems to me you girls spent a long time locked up in your rooms." Mrs. Salisbury sniffed suspiciously.

"Planning some kind of mischief, no doubt." Mr. Abbott wagged his finger playfully at the four girls.

George had a hard time keeping a straight face, and hastily took a sip of milk. Bess could not restrain a giggle, whereupon Mrs. Salisbury gave her a sharp look.

"Humph!" she exclaimed. "I must say I'll have to agree with Mr. Abbott this time. I'm sure you four *are* up to some prank."

Even Nancy and Joanne had to smother telltale grins. They only smiled pleasantly, but offered no explanation.

Actually, the girls were so excited over their

prospective adventure they could scarcely do justice to the excellent meal Mrs. Byrd had prepared. Karl Jr., as usual, was a charming companion.

He had many amusing anecdotes to tell, and Nancy was happy to observe that Joanne seemed to be enjoying it all immensely.

Indeed, by the time dessert was finished, Nancy and her chums realized that they had temporarily forgotten counterfeiters, syndicates, and even the nature cult on the hill.

Everyone was sorry, a little later, when the young man announced that he must leave.

"I wish I could stay," he said regretfully, letting his eyes rest especially long on Nancy, "but I must get back to the city tonight. I'll try to run down again in a few days to see Father. Take care of yourselves," he added to the girls.

After Karl Jr. had gone, and the girls were washing the dishes, George said teasingly, "You can't tell me 'Father' is the only attraction at Red Gate Farm! He has his eye on Nancy!"

"Silly!" Nancy laughed.

"He scarcely took his eyes off you all evening," George insisted. "You made quite a hit this morning with that rescued-heroine bit."

"Oh, honestly, George!" Nancy blushed. "You never give up, do you?"

"Karl Jr. wouldn't be so bad," Bess added,

"but imagine having Mr. Abbott for a father-in-law!"

"You do the imagining," Nancy said lightly. "I'm going outside and look at the hillside.".

All the girls watched until late in the evening, but the mysterious place remained dark and deserted. Disappointed, the girls went to bed.

They awakened early the next morning, for they had gradually become accustomed to farm hours. When they learned from Mrs. Byrd that Reuben was not feeling well, the girls eagerly helped with the various outdoor chores. It was noontime before they realized how much time had passed.

"You girls should have some relaxation this afternoon," Mrs. Byrd said. "How about a swim down in the brook? There's a spot that used to be known as the old swimming hole. It's fairly deep."

"That sounds wonderful," Bess declared.

Jo declined, but at two o'clock Nancy, Bess, and George set off in bathing suits. For two hours they swam, floated, and sun-bathed on the shore. Every once in a while Nancy or George would mention some angle of the colony, Hale Syndicate, or counterfeiting mysteries.

But immediately Bess would say, "Shush! We're relaxing. We may have a big night tonight."

Finally the girls started for the farmhouse. To reach it they had to cross a field in the corner of which lay a heap of large stones, apparently raked there when the acreage was cultivated.

George, grinning, climbed across the stones, saying, "This life is making me rugged. I— Oh, ouch!" she cried loudly, then added, "A snake! It bit me!"

CHAPTER XV

Masqueraders

NANCY and George turned just in time to see a brownish snake slither off in a wiggling motion and disappear among the stones.

"Oh, George!" Bess cried. "Was it a poisonous one?"

"I'm not sure," she answered, "I—I hope it wasn't a copperhead."

"We'd better not take any chances," Nancy declared, whipping a handkerchief from her beach robe. "Let's put on tourniquets, Bess."

Like lightning the two girls tied their handkerchiefs tightly above and below the puncture marks made in George's calf by the snake's fangs.

Then Nancy took a tiny pair of scissors from her bag. "I wish I had something to sterilize these with," she said.

"Will perfume do?" Bess asked, and took from her bag the tiny bottle of Blue Jade.

The liquid was poured onto the scissors, then Nancy deftly made a crosscut incision near the punctures. Blood spurted out, and with it, she hoped, any serum the snake might have injected.

George stoically had not made a sound, but finally she said, "Thanks, girls. Your quick first aid probably made it possible for me to go to the ceremonies tonight—if they have them."

"I think you'd better not step on your foot, or stimulate circulation," Nancy advised. "Suppose Bess and I carry you."

George started to protest but finally consented. Seated on a "chair" made by the intertwined hands of Nancy and Bess, George was carried toward the farmhouse.

The trip, though awkward and slow, went at a steady pace. George maintained her Spartan attitude. She not only refused to complain but teasingly asked Bess, "Aren't you glad I don't eat as much as you do?"

"I don't know what you mean," Bess replied, puzzled.

"Well, if I loved desserts as you do," George teased, "I wouldn't be such a featherweight to carry!"

Bess gave her cousin an indignant glance. "How do you like that for gratitude! Next time I lug you all the way home—!"

Nancy interrupted with a grin, "I guess we all do our share of eating dessert. Anyhow, we've made it, girls. Red Gate Farm is just ahead!"

As they came up to the house, Mrs. Salisbury, who was in the garden, exclaimed, "Oh, gracious! What happened?" Mr. Abbott and Mrs. Byrd hurried from the house.

"Just a precautionary measure," Nancy explained, and told of the snake incident.

George was carried indoors and laid on a couch. Mrs. Byrd quickly called the family physician. He arrived shortly, and examined George's wound.

The doctor nodded approvingly as he bathed it with an antiseptic and removed the tourniquets.

"Excellent first-aid treatment," he announced. "You'll be fine, young lady. I'd advise you to rest for several hours."

"Thank you. That's good news." George gave a relieved grin.

For the remainder of the afternoon she was made to lie inactive. When dinnertime came, George got up, declaring, "I never felt better!"

"But take it easy in case we go out tonight," Nancy pleaded with her.

To allay suspicion on the part of the other boarders, Bess and Joanne were posted as guards across the road. If they saw the beginning of rites on the hill, the girls were to give birdcalls. In the meantime, Nancy and George waited in George's room, the costumes ready to be picked up at a moment's notice.

Suddenly Nancy leaped from her chair and flew into her own bedroom. "What's eating you?" George called.

"Oh, why didn't I think of it before? How stupid of me!" Nancy said, returning with a piece of paper in her hand.

"What *are* you talking about?" George demanded.

"That snake today. The way he wriggled. It looked just like the mark over the numeral 2 in the coded message!" Nancy cried excitedly. "The 2 we think means B!"

George sat up. "You mean the B with the wavy line over it might signify the Black Snake Colony?"

"Yes. Oh, George, this connects the Hale Syndicate with the nature cult here. Now the message reads: "Maurice Hale calling Black Snake Colony meeting—"

"And the 18. How about that?" George asked.

"Not too hard to guess, George. The 18 is the letter R, and *could* stand for Red Gate Farm."

"Nancy, you're a whiz, as I've often told you," her friend declared.

The young sleuth smiled, then said wistfully, "If I could only have had another second to copy the next few numbers, I might have known the exact time."

"What happens now? Will you notify the police?"

At that instant Nancy and George heard soft birdcalls. "No time to phone now," Nancy said.

She grabbed two of the costumes and dashed from the room. George followed with the others. As prearranged, the girls left by the kitchen door to avoid the boarders. Mrs. Byrd had been told that the girls might go up the hillside to watch if the nature cult put on a performance.

Nancy and George joined the other girls and they all scurried toward the woods. It was very dark beneath the dense canopy of trees, and Bess gripped Nancy's arm. Joanne was familiar with every path and led the way toward the hillside.

A weird cry broke the stillness. Involuntarily the girls halted and moved closer together.

"What—was—that?" Bess chattered.

"Only some wild animal," Nancy reassured her. "Come on!" she urged. "We must hurry or we'll miss the ritual!"

The girls went through the dark forest as fast as they could. The moon was rising, and ghostly rays of light filtered through gaps in the foliage overhead. A faint breeze stirred the leaves into what seemed like menacing whispers. The girls finally reached the river trail and followed it.

"We must be careful now," Nancy warned in a low voice. "We're drawing near the colony. The cult may have a lookout stationed during the night ceremonies."

"I hadn't thought of that," Joanne murmured.

"I almost wish I hadn't come," Bess whispered nervously. "I had no idea it would be this dark."

"What were you expecting at nine-thirty at night?" George chided in as low a tone as possible.

"It will be lighter when the moon rises higher," Joanne told her. "Still—if you want to turn back—"

"No, I'm going through with this masquerade if the rest of you are!" Bess retorted stalwartly.

Nancy hoped fervently it would remain a masquerade. She was firmly convinced now that the Black Snake group were unscrupulous people working with, or at least friendly with Maurice Hale. Nancy now felt convinced that the mystic rites were nothing but a sham.

Fortunately, for Nancy's purpose, the hillside was covered with large rocks as well as dense shrubs which would provide temporary hiding places. As the girls stole cautiously up the steep path, they could see cult members still congregating.

"We're in plenty of time," she thought.

The girls separated, George and Bess crouching behind a huge rock. Joanne and Nancy took cover behind a heavy growth of shrubs and tall grass.

For nearly ten minutes the girls watched as figures milled about the hillside. Then they heard the sound of cars approaching.

"They must be coming up through the pasture again," Joanne said, listening intently.

An instant later she and Nancy saw the head-lights of three automobiles.

"Look!" Joanne tugged at Nancy's sleeve. "More members are coming out of their tents!"

The two girls watched the white-robed figures walking slowly toward the brow of the hill, where the three automobiles had parked.

"I wonder if one of the newcomers is Maurice Hale," Nancy thought.

She and Joanne were too far away to hear what was being said, but they could see distinctly. They watched as a group of men and women, twelve in number, stepped from the cars. Nancy could not distinguish any of their faces.

The new arrivals quickly donned white garments and headgear similar to the outfits Nancy and her friends had made, then joined the other members of the cult.

The ghostly figures soon began dancing about in the moonlight, and Nancy felt that the time was right for her daring attempt to join the group. Before she could tell Joanne, there was a slight stir in the bushes directly behind her.

Involuntarily Nancy jumped, fully expecting to come face to face with one of the cult members. Instead, Bess and George emerged.

"Isn't it about time for us to do something?" they asked, almost simultaneously.

"Yes," Nancy agreed, "we'd better get into our robes as quickly as we can."

The girls were well hidden by the rocks and bushes. They donned their costumes and pulled the headgear over their faces. For the first time, Nancy noticed the scent of Blue Jade on Bess. "I wonder if that was wise," Nancy thought. "If it attracts attention to Bess it might increase her danger, but it's too late now to do anything about it."

As George, overeager, started off, Nancy caught her friend's arm. "Wait!" she warned. "We must slip quietly into the circle one at a time."

"My knees are shaking now," Bess admitted. "I don't know how I'll be able to dance."

"Stay here if you like," Nancy told her. "I think we should leave someone to keep guard, anyway."

"I'll stay," Joanne offered. "I know the way back through the woods better than you girls do."

"Come on!" George pleaded. "If we don't hurry we'll be too late!"

"Good luck!" Joanne whispered as the girls crept away.

Inch by inch, the three girls made their way up the hill. They crouched behind a clump of bushes a stone's throw from where the cult members were dancing. Nancy indicated that she would make the first move. Bess and George nodded.

"The slightest mistake will mean detection!" Nancy thought, her heart pounding.

Waiting for the right moment, she suddenly slipped out among the white-robed figures and instantly began waving her arms and making grotesque motions.

CHAPTER XVI

Startling Commands

RELIEVED that her entry into the group had not been noticed, Nancy marched along with the other ghostly figures. If only George and Bess were as successful!

Nancy watched her disguised companions and saw that the girls would have no trouble in following the motions, since each person was apparently making them up on the spur of the moment.

"So far, so good," Nancy told herself.

Satisfied now that her own position was temporarily secure, she tried to help her friends. Deliberately moving toward the shrubs behind which George and Bess were hiding, she shielded them from the view of the cult members, all the time continuing her grotesque motions.

George realized what the young sleuth was trying to do and made the most of the opportunity. Choosing her time, she slipped out and joined the group on the hillside.

Bess was more timid. Several times at the critical moment she lost her nerve, but she finally managed to summon enough courage and made the plunge.

"Keep close together," Nancy warned in an undertone. "If we lose each other, it may be disastrous."

By this time the girls had made up their minds that there was nothing the least bit mystic about the queer rites of the Black Snake Colony. Disguised persons on all sides of them were making crude remarks which assured the girls that the cult members did not take the ceremony seriously.

"This ought to give the country yokels an eyeful!" Nancy heard one man mutter.

"How much longer do we have to do this?" another grumbled. "I'm getting sick of flapping my arms around like a windmill!"

"This cult idea was all foolishness, anyway!" still another said.

"Foolishness, is it?" someone caught him up. Nancy thought she recognized the voice but was not certain. "Let me tell you a girl was prowling around here only a few days ago! I guess the Chief knew his business when he thought up this crazy cult idea."

"Well, enough of this!" a loud voice announced. Nancy decided the man must be one of the leaders. "We may as well go into the cave and get down to business!"

George was just wondering what the girls had better do when Bess clutched Nancy's hand and whispered nervously:

"Do we dare enter?"

"We must," Nancy returned quietly.

The girls stood motionless, watching the white-robed figures march single file toward the entrance to the cave. Finally Nancy signaled, and the three friends followed the group, even though it occurred to them that they might be walking into a trap.

"Keep close behind me," Nancy warned her companions in a whisper.

As they approached the mouth of the opening, Nancy saw a tall figure, robed in white, standing guard. Her heart nearly stopped as she realized that each person was uttering some password.

"We're finished now," she thought.

It was too late to turn back. The three girls could do nothing but hope that in some way they might get past the stalwart guard.

Nancy kept close to the person just ahead of her, and as he muttered the password, she managed to hear it.

"Kamar!"

When Nancy's turn came to pass the guard, she spoke the word clearly. As she had hoped, George and Bess heard, and taking their cue from her, repeated the password. The sentry did not give them a second glance, yet the girls breathed easier when they were safely through the entrance.

The marchers descended into a cold, damp tunnel. Someone was carrying a torch at the head of the procession, but Nancy and her friends, who were near the end of the line, were in semidarkness.

"What do you suppose we're getting into?" George muttered.

Nancy did not reply, but gave her friend a sharp nudge as a warning not to speak. A moment later Bess tripped over some object in the path and would have fallen if Nancy had not caught her by the arm. They walked farther underground, and then, unexpectedly, stepped into a dimly lighted chamber.

The members of the cult seated themselves on the floor, and the girls followed their example. Presently they became aware of the strong scent of Blue Jade perfume. Bess was not the only one wearing it tonight!

"So there *is* a definite connection between this distinctive perfume and the Black Snake Colony!" Nancy thought. "No wonder that man on the train was startled. Perhaps the women use it,

and he couldn't identify me but took it for
granted I was one of the group. If so, it's just as
well Bess has some on."

Nancy suddenly recalled the forged note bear-
ing the Blue Jade scent. "The woman who delivered it to me must be a member of the cult!"
she thought excitedly.

After everyone had entered the room, the man
who had given the sharp order outside the cave
spoke again. He threw off his headgear and
glanced over the group appraisingly. Nancy was
stunned.

Maurice!

The man she had seen the first time she had
stopped at the filling station!

"Is he Maurice Hale?" she asked herself excitedly.

"Everyone here?" he demanded gruffly.

He counted the group, and again Nancy and
her friends held their breaths. Apparently some
of the members of the colony were missing, for
the leader did not notice that three new recruits
had been added to his organization.

"We may as well get down to work," the leader
announced. "Snead, have you anything to report?"

At the question one of the disguised persons
stood up and threw off his mask. Again Nancy was
startled. He was none other than the man she had
seen in Room 305!

"Here's the good money," he said, handing over an envelope. "Perfect score this time for our main distribution department."

"Very fine. Then nothing's gone wrong at your new office?"

"Not yet, Chief," was the muttered reply, "but yesterday I saw a bird hangin' around the building—looked like a plain-clothes cop to me. I don't want you to think I'm backing out, but if you ask me, I'd say it's about time to blow. This game can't last forever, you know."

"I'll do the thinking for this outfit!" the leader scathingly retorted. "We'll stay here another week and then pick a new spot. What makes you think the cops are wise?"

"Well, they may have got wise to the fact that we're using Yvonne again—"

"That's right!" a shrill, angry female voice interrupted. "Blame me! Every time somebody gets nervous, you bring me into it!"

Nancy could scarcely restrain herself. She had been right about Yvonne! The girl *was* mixed up in the Hale Syndicate racket!

"You deserve blame," Al Snead retorted irritably. "First, you didn't have any more sense than to sell a bottle of that perfume to a perfect stranger—"

"I told you, that girl insisted upon buying it, and I was afraid if I flatly refused, she and her friends would get suspicious. Besides, I don't see what harm it did to sell the perfume to a teen-ager!"

"No," Snead retorted sarcastically, "you're so simple-minded you wouldn't see it might land us in jail! When Pete was on the train going to River Heights he noticed the scent and thought that the girl was one of the Chief's agents! Lucky for all of us, he saw his mistake before he spilled anything!"

Yvonne sputtered back in defense. "Well, at least I phoned Al at his office right away so he could warn the agents about the stray bottle of Blue Jade. It's not *my* fault Pete happened to be on the same train as those girls."

The leader suddenly became impatient. "Enough of this!" he shouted. "It's not getting us anywhere! Snead, I placed Yvonne in your office and she'll stay there as long as I say. I'm satisfied with the rest of her work. Get me?"

Snead nodded sullenly.

Nancy had been studying the leader intently and by this time was convinced that he was far more clever and intelligent than his subordi-nates. She figured that Al Snead was right-hand man to the Chief, but resented his superior's favoritism toward Yvonne Wong. The organiza-tion was a large one, evidently changing its scene and type of operation from time to time. If only she could slip away and get help from the author-ities!

"Another thing," Al Snead continued, addressing Maurice Hale, "we'd better make up a new code. Those girls that have been gettin' too close to our operation just *might* notify the cops."

"All right," the Chief responded. "I'll work one out in a day or two."

He called on another member of the organization for a report. "Two hundred packages passed, sir."

"Good!" the leader exclaimed, rubbing his thin hands. "Now, if you'll follow me to the workroom, I'll give you each your cut, and dole out the stuff for next week."

Nancy and her friends could not have retreated had they wished, and certainly did not want to leave when they seemed so near the truth!

But the situation in which they found themselves was a foreboding one and the very atmosphere of the room was tense and frightening. Boldly they followed the others into an adjoining chamber which was brilliantly lighted with torches.

Though prepared for the unexpected, the girls were taken completely aback at the sight which greeted their eyes!

CHAPTER XVII

Tense Moments

NANCY's first impression on entering was that the chamber appeared to be a cross between a printing shop and a United States mint.

"Counterfeiters!" she thought excitedly.

Hand presses stood about and several engraved plates had been left on a table. Various chemicals and inks were in evidence. Neat stacks of paper money lined one wall and other bills were scattered carelessly on the floor. Never in all her life had Nancy seen so much money!

The room was cluttered with it. Twenty-dollar bills appeared to be everywhere. Money, still damp, was drying on tables. Nancy observed that all the bills seemed to be of the twenty-dollar denomination.

At last she had the answer to the many questions which had been troubling her! This was the secret of the cave! The latest racket of the

Hale Syndicate! The nature cult was a hoax, its so-called mysterious rites used only as a screen to hide the work of a clever band of counterfeiters! The Black Snake Colony seemed to her to be a perfect name.

Nancy realized that if she did not try to get away and bring help now, she and her friends would fail. There was nothing they could do by themselves.

Nancy turned to relay her intentions to Bess and George. A slight tug on their robes was all that was needed to make them understand, but to put the plan into operation was another matter.

The girls attempted to edge toward the chamber entrance by degrees, but Al Snead stood barring the door. For the time being escape was out of the question. They must bide their time.

As long as some members of the organization remained masked, the girls knew they would be comparatively safe. But already several people had stripped off their robes and headpieces. Every minute that the girls' escape was delayed increased the danger of detection.

Since it was impossible to sneak away, Nancy made careful note of her surroundings and tried to identify the faces on her mind. Except for Yvonne, the leader Maurice Hale, Al Snead, and the man she had seen on the train, all were strangers. Six people besides Bess, George, and herself remained masked.

As Nancy surveyed the elaborate equipment in the workroom, she realized that this was an unusually large gang of counterfeiters. The engraved plate which had been copied from an actual United States Government twenty-dollar bill was a work of art. Probably the leader of the gang had at one time been noted as a skilled engraver and had decided to use his talents to unlawful advantage.

Nancy carefully glanced about the room. Maurice Hale was looking over some stacks of counterfeit money while several members of the gang talked quietly. Bess and George automatically followed Nancy's gaze but stood perfectly still next to her near the table.

Nancy, under ordinary circumstances, could not have told the counterfeit money from the real thing—with the picture of Jackson on the face, and the White House on the back. But now that she had been alerted to examine the bills carefully, she noted that the color and texture of the paper appeared to be at fault.

When Nancy felt sure that she was not being observed, she stealthily picked up one of the bills and tucked it inside her robe as evidence.

"We made a pretty fair week's profit," Maurice Hale said gruffly as he stacked the bills into several large piles. You distributors and passers keep up like this for another month and I'd say we'll all be on Easy Street."

"The racket won't last another month," Al Snead growled. "I tell you, the federal agents are getting wise that the phony stuff's being passed around here."

"Bah!" Hale replied contemptuously. "Let them be suspicious! They wouldn't think of this out-of-the-way place as our headquarters in a thousand years!"

Nancy could not help but smile at his words. "That's what *he* thinks!"

The next voice that spoke startled Nancy. She recognized it instantly as belonging to Mr. Kent —the would-be buyer of Red Gate Farm!

"Yeah, maybe not," he was saying. "Still, it's too bad the old lady wouldn't sell her place. Then we'd really have a setup!"

It flashed through Nancy's mind that her hunch had been right about Mr. Kent being involved with the hillside cult. No wonder they wanted to obtain Red Gate Farm; it would have been a better headquarters for the gang than the cave.

The girl detective strained her ears as the conversation continued. A woman next to Kent said scornfully, "I only hope your bright idea about that fake letter we took to the Drew girl, and cutting the farm telephone wires, doesn't backfire."

So, Nancy told herself, it was Kent, and the woman who had just spoken, who were the ones responsible for that part of the mystery. Mr. Kent also was undoubtedly the driver of the car which had slowed down one evening near the farmhouse.

Meanwhile, the leader went on deftly stacking the money. Nancy and her friends watched him with increasing uneasiness. When the various members of the organization were called upon to accept their share of the counterfeit bills, they would doubtless remove their masks. How would the girls escape detection then?

Nancy realized the situation was becoming more serious. She and her friends must escape before the actual distribution of the money began. If only Al Snead would move away from the door!

One thought comforted Nancy. Joanne was on guard outside the cave. If worst came to worst and escape was cut off, Joanne undoubtedly would become alarmed and hurry back to the farmhouse for help.

"We may have to make a dash for it!" Nancy warned George in a whisper. "If that man moves away from the door, be ready!"

Al Snead did not move, however, and it seemed to the girls that he was watching them. They wondered if their whispering had made him suspicious.

Bess trembled slightly, and moved nearer Nancy. Maurice Hale had finished counting the money, and, glancing over the assembly, announced in a commanding voice:

"Well, those of you who haven't removed your masks had better do it one by one. I want to be sure no one is here who shouldn't be!" He pointed to Bess. "You first!"

Nancy and her friends felt themselves go cold. They were trapped! There was nothing they could do now but make a wild dash for safety.

"Ready!" Nancy muttered under her breath.

Before the girls could put their ideas into action, they were startled by a loud commotion in the tunnel. An instant later the guard, who had been stationed at the entrance of the cave, burst into the chamber. He was half dragging a young girl who fought violently to free herself.

The victim was Joanne!

CHAPTER XVIII

Prisoners

NANCY's first impulse was to dash forward and try to help Joanne. But instantly she realized the foolishness of such an act. George half started toward Joanne, but Nancy restrained her.

"Wait!" she whispered tensely.

If the situation had been grave before, it was even more serious now. With Joanne captured there was no one to go for help! The girls must depend entirely on themselves to escape from the cave. No one at the farmhouse knew that they were doing anything more than watching the Black Snake Colony from a safe distance.

"Let me go!" Joanne cried, struggling to free herself.

"Where did she come from?" Maurice Hale demanded unpleasantly.

"I saw her hiding among the bushes," the guard informed him. "She was spying! But she got just a little too curious!"

"Spying, eh?" A harsh expression crossed the leader's face. "Well, we know what to do with snoopers!"

"It's all a mistake," Joanne murmured, on the verge of tears. "I didn't mean any harm. I'm Mrs. Byrd's granddaughter and I was merely curious to know more about the cult."

Even as Joanne spoke, her eyes traveled about the room, noting the stacks of money and the queer printing presses. She tried not to show that she understood their significance, but it was too late. The leader had seen her startled expression.

"So?" he drawled smartly. "This time your curiosity has been the means of getting you into serious trouble. You'll learn, by the time we get through with you, not to meddle in affairs that don't concern you!" He turned quickly to Snead. "Al, see that no one leaves this room!"

"Yes, Chief," the guard answered.

Nancy wondered what he had in mind. Just then Maurice Hale continued in a cold, harsh voice:

"Just to make sure that other spies haven't been pulling a fast one on us, I'll have everyone remove his mask at once. Be mighty quick about it too!"

"No!" Bess whimpered aloud. Then, realizing what she had done, she covered her mouth and sank back against the wall.

All heads turned in her direction. Nancy and

her friends had deliberately delayed in removing their masks, but now Nancy knew their effort to gain time was doomed.

With Al Snead still blocking the door, things looked black. Most of the others already had stripped off their headgear.

In addition to Maurice Hale and Al Snead, Nancy immediately recognized Yvonne Wong and Pete, the man who had spoken to her on the train. Next she spotted Mr. Kent, and finally, the woman with the upswept hairdo who had brought her the faked letter.

"That woman's the same one I saw at the service station with the three men," Nancy thought. "If she hadn't changed her hair style, I might have recognized her the night she delivered the note."

The other unmasked members were strangers to Nancy. Tensely now she watched as the leader stood before Bess.

"Nothing to be afraid of, dear," he said, and gently lifted off the ghostly head covering. The next instant Maurice Hale practically shrieked, "A spy!"

His face contorted with rage, Maurice snatched the white cloth headpieces from George's face, then Nancy's. Their scheme was exposed to all the members of the counterfeit gang!

For an instant there was stunned silence, then

angry cries arose from the Black Snake Colony members.

"They're the ones who bought the Blue Jade perfume from me!" Yvonne Wong shrieked.

Al Snead glared at Nancy. "Yeah. I knew something was wrong when you came into the office wearin' the Blue Jade. I smelled it, but didn't let on."

He then pointed accusingly toward Joanne. "That girl is the one who applied at our city office for a job! When she told me who she was and where she was from I knew she was the last person in the world we'd want to hire!"

"That crazy idea of yours about someone with farm experience," the leader cried. "We didn't need anybody to talk to our agents about cows and chickens—"

"But this place *is* in the country," Al Snead defended himself. "And in our codes we use a lot of that kind of lingo."

"Silence!" Maurice yelled, and turned to Joanne. "So you thought you'd get a job at our office and spy on us! And your meddling friend Nancy Drew was in cahoots with you."

"No, oh no!" Joanne cried out. "It was only by accident. I wanted to find a job and help my grandmother. Nancy was just trying to help me locate the office—"

"Don't expect us to believe a trumped-up story

like that," the leader said harshly. "We know all about why you two have been snooping around ever since Al had Pete trail you from Riverside Heights. What's more, we know how to deal with such people!"

Hale turned menacingly to Nancy. "You'll wish you'd taken Pete's advice when he called your pal"—he indicated George—"and warned her that you'd better mind your own business."

"Oh, Maurice, please don't be too harsh with the girls," a timid voice pleaded. "They didn't mean any harm." As she finished, the speaker removed her mask.

Nancy turned quickly to see the woman she had helped in the woods and later had taken to town.

"So she's a counterfeiter!" Nancy told herself incredulously. "I can't believe it!"

"Didn't mean any harm?" Maurice drawled sarcastically. "Oh, no, of course not. They only wanted to land the whole Hale Syndicate in jail! Not that you would care! If I had known what a whiner you are, I'd never have married you! Mind your own business and let me take care of this!"

In spite of the seriousness of her own situation, Nancy felt pity for the woman. Undoubtedly as the wife of such a tyrant as Maurice Hale she had stayed with him against her will. She had hated the life that he had forced her to lead, but evidently she had been powerless to escape from it.

"No wonder the poor woman took a chance and slipped away from time to time," Nancy thought.

Frightened by the harsh words of her husband, Mrs. Hale moved back into a far corner of the room. Nancy wished she could help her in some way, but realized that the woman dared not say more.

"What'll we do with these girls?" the leader demanded. "We can't let 'em go. They know too much!"

On all sides angry mutterings arose. Yvonne Wong heartlessly proposed that the girls be tied up and left prisoners in the cave. But Maurice Hale ruled down that suggestion.

"We'll have to get 'em out of here," he said. "They'll be missed and a searching party might visit this joint. How about the shack at the river? It's in such a desolate spot no one would think of looking there until after—"

He did not finish the sentence, but from the sinister expression on his face, Nancy and her friends guessed his meaning. He intended to lock them up in the cabin and leave them without food!

A cry of anguish came from the leader's wife. Rushing forward, she clutched her husband frantically by the arm.

"Oh, Maurice! You couldn't be that cruel!"

Mr. Hale flung her away from him with a force that sent the woman reeling against the wall. She uttered a little moan of pain and sank to the floor.

"Oh!" Bess screamed.

Even the cult members were startled.

"Be quiet!" ordered their chief.

The cruel action aroused Nancy. For an instant all eyes were centered on the woman, and Nancy thought she saw her opportunity. Quick as a flash she made a rush for the exit. Bess and George, equally alert, darted after her.

Al Snead, who stood in the opening, was taken completely by surprise. He tried to hold his ground but the girls were too strong for him. He managed to detain Bess and George, but Nancy wriggled from his grasp. She hesitated when she saw her friends had failed.

"Go on, Nancy!" Bess shrieked. "You must escape!"

Nancy darted into the next room, while George and Bess struggled with their captor, trying to block the door and give their friend more time.

"Stop that girl!" Maurice Hale shouted angrily. "If you let her get away, I'll—"

Nancy plunged into the tunnel and was swallowed up by darkness. She ran for her life and for the lives of her friends, realizing this probably was her only chance.

The long white robe hindered her, but there

"Go on, Nancy!" Bess shrieked.
"You must escape!"

was no time to tear it off. She held it high above her knees. Once she stumbled, but caught herself, and rushed on frantically.

The tunnel seemed to have no end. Behind her, Nancy could hear pounding footsteps and angry shouts. She thought the men must be gaining. If only she could reach the mouth of the cave!

The tunnel wound in and out and several times Nancy brushed against the rough stone wall. The route was so circuitous that she began to think she had taken a wrong turn.

Then, just as she was giving up hope, Nancy spotted a dim light far ahead and knew she must be nearing the mouth of the cave. No one appeared to be left guarding the entrance. Her only chance! In a moment more she had reached the open air.

"Saved!" Nancy breathed.

At that instant a dark figure loomed up from the grass. Nancy felt a heavy hand on her shoulder!

CHAPTER XIX

Destroyed Evidence

"NOT SO FAST there!" The man leered as he clutched Nancy firmly by the arm and whirled her around. "What's the big rush, anyway?"

Nancy, staring into his hard face, saw that he was the man who had been addressed as "Hank," one of the three men she had seen at the filling station. Frantically she struggled to free herself.

"So—" he muttered in satisfaction, "the pretty blond spy the boys were telling me about. I thought you were warned by the guard to keep away from here! This time, I take it, you're lookin' for something besides a stray cow!"

"Yes, and I'm going to find it!" Nancy said bravely.

"Oh, yeah? You're going to find what? The police?" Hank looked at her costume. "You're a spy. But your little game is up."

Nancy's pulse was racing. How could she get

away? She could hear running footsteps coming through the tunnel, and knew her chance of escape would be over in another instant. In desperation she tried to jerk herself free from Hank. But her captor gripped her more securely and laughed as she cried out in pain.

"Let me go!"

Nancy twisted and squirmed, but her efforts only made Hank tighten his grip. By the time the others reached her, she had given up the struggle and stood quietly waiting for the worst to come.

"Good thing you got her, Hank," Maurice Hale called. "The little wildcat! We'll give her a double dose for this smart trick! No girl's going to put anything over on me!"

At the entrance of the cave it was nearly as bright as day, for the moon was high. Maurice Hale glanced nervously about, as though fearing observation by unseen eyes.

"Get back inside!" he sharply ordered his followers. "It's a clear night and some wise bird might see us without our costumes and wonder what's up. We must destroy the evidence as quickly as we can and clear out of this place!"

Even as the leader spoke, Nancy thought she heard a rustling in the nearby bushes. She told herself that it probably was only the wind stirring the leaves. Rescue was out of the question, for no one knew that she and her friends had planned such a dangerous mission. How foolish, of them not to have revealed their full plans to someone!

Nancy made no protest as she was dragged back into the cavern. Bravely she tried to meet the eyes of her friends, for she saw that they were even more discouraged than she. Poor Bess was trembling with fright.

"Th-the perfume did it!" she wailed. "I knew this masquerade was far too dangerous for us to try!"

"Cheer up," Nancy whispered encouragingly. "We'll find some way to get out of here!"

Bess only shook her head. She was not to be deceived.

"And to think *I* was the one who couldn't wait for a spooky adventure on the hillside," George moaned regretfully. "I really ought to have my head examined!"

The members of the syndicate were furious. There would be no second opportunity for these intruders to break away. At an order from the leader, Al Snead found several pieces of rope and bound Nancy and her friends hand and foot. He seemed to take particular delight in making Nancy's bonds cruelly tight.

"I guess that'll hold you for a while." He grinned, gloating over the girls' predicament.

"Get to work!" the leader commanded his men impatiently. "Do you think we have the rest of the night? If we don't hurry up and get out of here, the cops are apt to be down on us! Don't know what this girl's done."

All colony members, except Mrs. Hale, went to work with a will; the fear of the law obviously had affected them. With a sinking heart, Nancy realized the men planned to destroy all the evidence of their counterfeiting operations.

"The machines that we can't take with us we'll wreck," Maurice Hale ordered. "If we save the plates we can start up again in a new place. Get a move on!"

He stood over the men, driving them furiously. His wife had slumped down in a chair and had buried her face in her hands. She appeared crushed. Only once did she summon her energy to speak.

"Maurice," she murmured brokenly, "why won't you give up this dreadful life—always running from the police? We were happy before you got mixed up with such bad company."

Her husband cut her short with a sarcastic remark. She did not try to speak again, but sat hunched over, looking sorrowfully at the girls. Nancy knew that she wanted to help them, but did not have the courage for further defiance.

The work of destroying the counterfeiting machinery went on, but several times Maurice Hale glanced impatiently at his watch.

"No use waiting until we're through here," he observed after a time. "Let's get the prisoners out of here pronto. The sooner we're rid of them, the safer I'll feel. Al, you start on ahead with one of the automobiles. You know the way to the shack, don't you?"

"Sure," Al Snead agreed promptly.

"Then take Hank along to keep guard and get going!"

Nancy and her chums were jerked to their feet. The cords around their ankles were removed to permit them to walk, but their arms were kept tied securely behind them.

"Move along!" Al Snead ordered Nancy, giving her a hard shove forward.

The girls stumbled along through the dark passageway from the inner room to the mouth of the cave. Men and women followed them with angry, menacing threats.

Al and Hank pushed the girls to make them hurry. Nancy and her friends exchanged hopeless glances from time to time. George held her head up contemptuously, but Joanne was white as a sheet and Bess was on the verge of tears.

"Guess this'll teach you girls to mix with the Black Snake Colony!" a raucous voice said as the group made its way toward the exit.

Nancy held back a retort, but her icy look told the man she did not appreciate the remark. Their walk seemed interminable. Finally, however, moonlight could be seen. In a moment they were approaching the mouth of the cave.

Nancy took a few halting steps and then paused as if she had turned to stone. Her eyes were riveted upon the entrance. There stood Mr. Abbott's son, Karl Jr.!

"Oh, Karl!" Nancy cried out. "These men are counterfeiters! Don't let them capture you too! Run!"

CHAPTER XX

A Final Hunch

KARL ABBOTT did not run. Instead, he signaled with his hand. At once seven armed men sprang from the darkness of nearby bushes.

"Secret Service agents," Karl explained quickly to the girls.

"Stand where you are! Don't anyone move!" ordered one of the federal men.

So unexpected was their arrival that the counterfeiters were stunned. For an instant no one moved. Then, with a cry of rage, Maurice Hale darted into the cavern. He had taken only a few steps when one of the other agents grabbed him firmly by one arm.

"None of that! We have you right this time, Hale. You won't try any funny stuff with Uncle Sam again!"

Some of the counterfeiters who had not yet come from the cavern had turned back.

"They'll get away through the other exit!" Nancy cried out.

Karl smiled. "We have that covered too."

He now introduced the four girls to Secret Service Agent Horton who was in charge of the group. The federal man gave Nancy Drew a quick word of praise for revealing the headquarters of the counterfeiting ring.

"Outwitted—by that snooping kid!" Maurice Hale screamed.

The thought seemed to unnerve the man completely. He did not protest when handcuffs were put on his wrists. Other members of the syndicate submitted to the agents without resistance, although Yvonne Wong vehemently protested her innocence.

"I didn't know what it was all about until tonight," she cried angrily. "It isn't fair to arrest me! I've worked for Mr. Snead only a few days—"

"You'll have to think up a better story than that!" she was told bluntly. "Your name has been mixed up in underhanded deals before, but this is the first time we've been able to get any evidence against you."

While the prisoners were being rounded up, Karl Abbott rushed over to the girls and quickly freed their hands.

"Are you all right?" he asked anxiously.

"Yes," Nancy told him, "but if you hadn't arrived just when you did, it might have been a different story!"

She was on the verge of asking what had brought him to the cave at the psychological moment when she saw that two federal agents were placing handcuffs on the wrists of Maurice Hale's wife. Breaking away from her friends, Nancy darted to the other side of the room.

"Oh, don't arrest Mrs. Hale," she pleaded. "She isn't like the rest. She tried to save us, but they wouldn't listen to her."

"Sorry," Horton returned, "but we'll have to take her along. If you want to intercede for her later, we may be able to have her sentence lightened."

After the prisoners had been herded out of the cave to waiting government automobiles and the printing plates used in the making of the counterfeit bills had been collected, Nancy felt explanations were in order from Karl.

"How did you know we had come here?" Nancy asked him.

"From Mrs. Byrd. She was greatly worried. When I came to see Father tonight she told me that after you'd gone she found evidence of your costume making. She confided in me you might have done just what you did. She asked me to try and stop you."

"Yes. Go on," Nancy urged.

"Well, I've been suspicious of this hillside

ceremony stuff, and after talking further with
Mrs. Byrd, I decided to get in touch with the
Secret Service men she said you had told her
about. They couldn't come, but the chief agent
in this area sent some of his other men."

"How marvelous of you to have put two and
two together!" Bess exclaimed.

"By the time we all got here," Karl went on,
"no one was around. I sneaked inside just as all
of you were coming out. Mr. Horton thought you
girls would not be harmed if you walked outside
before the gang was captured."

"Thanks for that," said George. "I've had
enough!"

Just then Secret Service Agent Horton came
over to Nancy's group and extended his hand to
her. "Miss Drew," he said earnestly, "I want to
thank you for your work which has resulted in
the solution of one of the most baffling cases of
counterfeiting the United States Government has
ever had. How did you do it?"

Nancy blushed at the praise. "It was sort of a
chain reaction, I guess," the young sleuth replied,
and told of the various circumstances that had led
to tonight's adventure.

When she finished, the agent shook his head in
amazement. "You cracked a code this gang had
thought was unbreakable. My congratulations."

It was late when the four girls, escorted by
Karl Abbott, left the cave. As they neared the

farmhouse, Joanne observed that the lights were on. "I hope Gram hasn't been too worried."

Before the girls reached the porch, Mrs. Byrd came hurrying toward them. She clung tightly to Joanne for an instant.

"I'm so glad you're back," she murmured in relief. "And you girls are all right. I was terribly afraid those members of the Black Snake Colony—"

She was interrupted by Mrs. Salisbury's voice from the dark porch. "You had us so worried we couldn't go to bed. The idea of girls running around the country at this hour! That nature cult is all foolishness, anyway!"

"Absolutely!" Mr. Abbott agreed. "The less you meddle with their affairs, the wiser you'll be!"

"You're wrong this time, Father," Karl Jr. announced. "If the girls hadn't meddled, those counterfeiters would have operated indefinitely."

"Counterfeiters!" the two boarders and Mrs. Byrd exclaimed together.

They were tense as Karl Jr. related everything that had happened. In fact, it was not until the next day that Mrs. Salisbury recovered from the shock sufficiently to boast:

"Well, I always said those girls were up and coming!"

Mr. Abbott was very proud of the part his son had played in the case, and said so several times.

Mrs. Byrd had nothing except praise for Nancy and her friends. "And who would think," she said incredulously, "that Bess's innocent purchase of a bottle of perfume would lead you girls to a mystery right here at Red Gate Farm!"

However, the removal of the Black Snake Colony from her property left her a serious financial problem. "I'm glad they're gone," she said, "but I'll miss the money. I can't hope to rent the land again. It isn't fertile enough for farming. All this talk about counterfeiters is apt to give Red Gate a bad name, too. I'll probably lose those other boarders who were coming!"

"Publicity is a queer thing," Nancy said thoughtfully. "Sometimes one can work it to one's advantage. That's what we'll do now."

"How?" Joanne asked.

"We'll advertise that counterfeiters' cavern to sightseers and make enough money to lift a dozen mortgages!"

The others were enthusiastic. During the next week the girls, with Karl Jr.'s assistance, placed in the cave for public display an imitation setup of the counterfeiting operation. There were several old printing presses, and some dummy figures arranged before them as if "at work." Scattered about the cave floor were stacks of homemade "money"—to represent counterfeit bills.

The following week Mr. Drew came to Red Gate Farm. A few miles away he halted his automobile at the side of the road, and with an amused smile studied a large billboard which read:

Follow the arrow to Red Gate Farm! See the mysterious cavern used by counterfeiters! Admission fifty cents.

As Carson Drew continued slowly in his car, he presently came to another sign, bolder than the first:

Regain health at Red Gate Farm. Boarders by Day or Week.

The traffic was unusually heavy, and the lawyer soon realized that all of the cars were headed for the farm. The place was crowded. He parked as near the house as he could and walked up the path. The grounds were well kept and equipped with swings and huge umbrellas. A number of persons, evidently boarders, were enjoying the garden.

Before Carson Drew had reached the front door, it was flung open, and Nancy rushed to meet him. "Dad!" she cried joyfully. "Isn't this wonderful?"

"You've done a magnificent job, Nancy."

After a hearty dinner Nancy and her friends took Mr. Drew to the hillside cave. Reuben Ames, looking most unlike himself in a new suit which was a trifle too tight, was in his glory as he conducted groups of visitors through the cavern.

"I've collected thirty dollars already today," he hailed Nancy as she came up with her friends. "This beats plowin' corn."

Bess grinned. "Didn't I always say that adventure follows Nancy Drew around?"

And Bess was right, for another exciting adventure awaited her courageous friend, who very soon was to become involved in *The Clue in the Diary*.

Mr. Drew laughed. "Nancy," he said, "as I think of your adventure at Red Gate Farm I can't decide whether you're better as a detective or as a promoter!"

Order Form
Own the original 58 action-packed
THE HARDY BOYS® MYSTERY STORIES

In *hardcover* at your local bookseller OR
simply mail in this handy order coupon and start your collection today!

Please send me the following Hardy Boys titles I've checked below.

All Books Priced @ $5.99

AVOID DELAYS   Please Print Order Form Clearly

❑	1	Tower Treasure	448-08901-7	❑ 30	Wailing Siren Mystery	448-08930-0
❑	2	House on the Cliff	448-08902-5	❑ 31	Secret of Wildcat Swamp	448-08931-9
❑	3	Secret of the Old Mill	448-08903-3	❑ 32	Crisscross Shadow	448-08932-7
❑	4	Missing Chums	448-08904-1	❑ 33	The Yellow Feather Mystery	448-08933-5
❑	5	Hunting for Hidden Gold	448-08905-X	❑ 34	The Hooded Hawk Mystery	448-08934-3
❑	6	Shore Road Mystery	448-08906-8	❑ 35	The Clue in the Embers	448-08935-1
❑	7	Secret of the Caves	448-08907-6	❑ 36	The Secret of Pirates Hill	448-08936-X
❑	8	Mystery of Cabin Island	448-08908-4	❑ 37	Ghost at Skeleton Rock	448-08937-8
❑	9	Great Airport Mystery	448-08909-2	❑ 38	Mystery at Devil's Paw	448-08938-6
❑	10	What Happened at Midnight	448-08910-6	❑ 39	Mystery of the Chinese Junk	448-08939-4
❑	11	While the Clock Ticked	448-08911-4	❑ 40	Mystery of the Desert Giant	448-08940-8
❑	12	Footprints Under the Window	448-08912-2	❑ 41	Clue of the Screeching Owl	448-08941-6
❑	13	Mark on the Door	448-08913-0	❑ 42	Viking Symbol Mystery	448-08942-4
❑	14	Hidden Harbor Mystery	448-08914-9	❑ 43	Mystery of the Aztec Warrior	448-08943-2
❑	15	Sinister Sign Post	448-08915-7	❑ 44	The Haunted Fort	448-08944-0
❑	16	A Figure in Hiding	448-08916-5	❑ 45	Mystery of the Spiral Bridge	448-08945-9
❑	17	Secret Warning	448-08917-3	❑ 46	Secret Agent on Flight 101	448-08946-7
❑	18	Twisted Claw	448-08918-1	❑ 47	Mystery of the Whale Tattoo	448-08947-5
❑	19	Disappearing Floor	448-08919-X	❑ 48	The Arctic Patrol Mystery	448-08948-3
❑	20	Mystery of the Flying Express	448-08920-3	❑ 49	The Bombay Boomerang	448-08949-1
❑	21	The Clue of the Broken Blade	448-08921-1	❑ 50	Danger on Vampire Trail	448-08950-5
❑	22	The Flickering Torch Mystery	448-08922-X	❑ 51	The Masked Monkey	448-08951-3
❑	23	Melted Coins	448-08923-8	❑ 52	The Shattered Helmet	448-08952-1
❑	24	Short-Wave Mystery	448-08924-6	❑ 53	The Clue of the Hissing Serpent	448-08953-X
❑	25	Secret Panel	448-08925-4	❑ 54	The Mysterious Caravan	448-08954-8
❑	26	The Phantom Freighter	448-08926-2	❑ 55	The Witchmaster's Key	448-08955-6
❑	27	Secret of Skull Mountain	448-08927-0	❑ 56	The Jungle Pyramid	448-08956-4
❑	28	The Sign of the Crooked Arrow	448-08928-9	❑ 57	The Firebird Rocket	448-08957-2
❑	29	The Secret of the Lost Tunnel	448-08929-7	❑ 58	The Sting of the Scorpion	448-08958-0

Also Available: The Hardy Boys Detective Handbook 448-01990-6
The Bobbsey Twins of Lakeport 448-09071-6

VISIT PENGUIN PUTNAM BOOKS FOR YOUNG READERS ONLINE:
http://www.penguinputnam.com/yreaders/index.htm

Payable in US funds only. Postage & handling: US/Can. $2.75 for one book, $1.00 for each add'l book not to exceed $6.75; Int'l $5.00 for one book, $1.00 for each add'l. We accept Visa, MC, AMEX ($10.00 min.), checks ($15.00 fee for returned checks), and money orders. No Cash/COD. Call (800) 788-6262 or (201) 933-9292, fax (201) 896-8569, or mail your orders to:

Penguin Putnam Inc.	Bill my
PO Box 12289 Dept. B	credit card # _____exp.____
Newark, NJ 07101-5289	___ Visa ___ MC ___ AMEX
	Signature: _____

Bill to: _____	Book Total $_____
Address _____	
City _____ ST _____ ZIP_____	Applicable sales tax $_____
Daytime phone #_____	
	Postage & Handling $_____
Ship to:_____	
Address_____	Total amount due $_____
City _____ ST _____ ZIP_____	

Please allow 4–6 weeks for US delivery. Can./Int'l orders please allow 6–8 weeks.
This offer is subject to change without notice.   Ad # ____

NANCY DREW MYSTERY STORIES®, THE HARDY BOYS®, and THE BOBBSEY TWINS® are trademarks of
Simon & Schuster, Inc., and are registered in the United States Patent and Trademark Office.

Order Form
Own the original 56 thrilling
NANCY DREW MYSTERY STORIES®

In *hardcover* at your local bookseller OR
simply mail in this handy order coupon and start your collection today!

Please send me the following Nancy Drew titles I've checked below.
All Books Priced @ $5.99

AVOID DELAYS   Please Print Order Form Clearly

❏	1 Secret of the Old Clock	448-09501-7	❏	30 Clue of the Velvet Mask	448-09530-0
❏	2 Hidden Staircase	448-09502-5	❏	31 Ringmaster's Secret	448-09531-9
❏	3 Bungalow Mystery	448-09503-3	❏	32 Scarlet Slipper Mystery	448-09532-7
❏	4 Mystery at Lilac Inn	448-09504-1	❏	33 Witch Tree Symbol	448-09533-5
❏	5 Secret of Shadow Ranch	448-09505-X	❏	34 Hidden Window Mystery	448-09534-3
❏	6 Secret of Red Gate Farm	448-09506-8	❏	35 Haunted Showboat	448-09535-1
❏	7 Clue in the Diary	448-09507-6	❏	36 Secret of the Golden Pavilion	448-09536-X
❏	8 Nancy's Mysterious Letter	448-09508-4	❏	37 Clue in the Old Stagecoach	448-09537-8
❏	9 The Sign of the Twisted Candles	448-09509-2	❏	38 Mystery of the Fire Dragon	448-09538-6
❏	10 Password to Larkspur Lane	448-09510-6	❏	39 Clue of the Dancing Puppet	448-09539-4
❏	11 Clue of the Broken Locket	448-09511-4	❏	40 Moonstone Castle Mystery	448-09540-8
❏	12 The Message in the Hollow Oak	448-09512-2	❏	41 Clue of the Whistling Bagpipes	448-09541-6
❏	13 Mystery of the Ivory Charm	448-09513-0	❏	42 Phantom of Pine Hill	448-09542-4
❏	14 The Whispering Statue	448-09514-9	❏	43 Mystery of the 99 Steps	448-09543-2
❏	15 Haunted Bridge	448-09515-7	❏	44 Clue in the Crossword Cipher	448-09544-0
❏	16 Clue of the Tapping Heels	448-09516-5	❏	45 Spider Sapphire Mystery	448-09545-9
❏	17 Mystery of the Brass-Bound Trunk	448-09517-3	❏	46 The Invisible Intruder	448-09546-7
❏	18 Mystery at Moss-Covered Mansion	448-09518-1	❏	47 The Mysterious Mannequin	448-09547-5
❏	19 Quest of the Missing Map	448-09519-X	❏	48 The Crooked Banister	448-09548-3
❏	20 Clue in the Jewel Box	448-09520-3	❏	49 The Secret of Mirror Bay	448-09549-1
❏	21 The Secret in the Old Attic	448-09521-1	❏	50 The Double Jinx Mystery	448-09550-5
❏	22 Clue in the Crumbling Wall	448-09522-X	❏	51 Mystery of the Glowing Eye	448-09551-3
❏	23 Mystery of the Tolling Bell	448-09523-8	❏	52 The Secret of the Forgotten City	448-09552-1
❏	24 Clue in the Old Album	448-09524-6	❏	53 The Sky Phantom	448-09553-X
❏	25 Ghost of Blackwood Hall	448-09525-4	❏	54 The Strange Message	
❏	26 Clue of the Leaning Chimney	448-09526-2		in the Parchment	448-09554-8
❏	27 Secret of the Wooden Lady	448-09527-0	❏	55 Mystery of Crocodile Island	448-09555-6
❏	28 The Clue of the Black Keys	448-09528-9	❏	56 The Thirteenth Pearl	448-09556-4
❏	29 Mystery at the Ski Jump	448-09529-7			

VISIT PENGUIN PUTNAM BOOKS FOR YOUNG READERS ONLINE:
http://www.penguinputnam.com/yreaders/index.htm

Payable in US funds only. Postage & handling: US/Can. $2.75 for one book, $1.00 for each add'l book not to exceed $6.75; Int'l $5.00 for one book, $1.00 for each add'l. We accept Visa, MC, AMEX ($10.00 min.), checks ($15.00 fee for returned checks), and money orders. No Cash/COD. Call (800) 788-6262 or (201) 933-9292, fax (201) 896-8569, or mail your orders to:

Penguin Putnam Inc.
PO Box 12289 Dept. B
Newark, NJ 07101-5289

Bill my
credit card # _____ exp. ____
___ Visa ___ MC ___ AMEX
Signature: _____

Bill to: _____
Address _____
City _____ ST _____ ZIP _____
Daytime phone # _____

Ship to: _____
Address _____
City _____ ST _____ ZIP _____

Book Total $ _____

Applicable sales tax $ _____

Postage & Handling $ _____

Total amount due $ _____

Please allow 4–6 weeks for US delivery. Can./Int'l orders please allow 6–8 weeks.
This offer is subject to change without notice.   Ad # ____

NANCY DREW MYSTERY STORIES®, THE HARDY BOYS®, AND THE BOBBSEY TWINS® are trademarks of
Simon & Schuster, Inc., and are registered in the United States Patent and Trademark Office.